# ADVANCE

"Michal Lemberger is a wonderful writer—empathetic and heartbreaking, generous and fierce. The searing beauty of these stories is matched only by the passion and intelligence of the women who inhabit these pages. *After Abel* is a stunning book."

—MOLLY ANTOPOL,
author of *The UnAmericans*

"Through intuition and art, Lemberger opens our hearts to the powerful women of the Bible. They come alive in her magical prose, and their wisdom, long stifled and marginalized, echoes across the millennia to warm our hearts and to illumine our turbulent age. They teach us not only how to survive, but how to thrive."

—RABBI BRADLEY SHAVIT ARTSON, Abner and
Roslyn Goldstine Dean's Chair of the Ziegler School
of Rabbinic Studies at the American Jewish University
and author of *God of Becoming and Relationship:
The Dynamic Nature of Process Theology*

"What struck me most about these stories is their clear, assured confidence—as if Michal had pulled apart some of the lines in the old story, spied a new story tucked in there way off in a corner, shimmied in a fishhook and pulled it

"*After Abel* brings biblical women from the sidelines to the center of the story, in a compelling narrative reminiscent of Anita Diamant's *The Red Tent*. These beautifully written stories feel like meeting Eve, Lot's wife, and many other compelling characters for the first time. Michal Lemberger—more, please!"

—LAUREL CORONA, author of *The Mapmaker's Daughter, Finding Emilie,* and *Penelope's Daughter*

"The Bible is predominantly a set of books by and about men, with women usually mentioned only peripherally. In *After Abel,* Lemberger portrays biblical women in a way that makes them come alive as real people, with perspectives, concerns, and emotions of their own. Her modern midrash is true to all the biblical stories but enhances them in a way that I never thought possible. This may not have been how these biblical women actually thought and felt, but it probably was!"

—RABBI ELLIOT DORFF, Rector and Distinguished Professor of Philosophy at the American Jewish University and author of *The Unfolding Tradition: Philosophies of Jewish Law*

"This is a beautiful book of modern midrash—the ancient Jewish tradition of telling the stories between the Hebrew Bible's lines. The women I thought I knew have come alive in these gorgeous and captivating stories, and they are unlike anything I expected. Their bravery and radiance remained in my mind long after I finished reading."

—DARA HORN, winner of the National Jewish Book Award and author of *A Guide for the Perplexed* and *The World to Come*

"This is such an unusual book—how shall we begin to think of women behind the stentorian voices of the men who rule the scriptures—to think of them cooking slaughtered animals and caring for the children, to think of them being instructed constantly about how to behave, to live, to obey... who can possibly guess now what their real-time lives were like? Lemberger does a heroic job. What she gives us is an idea of what real women—women not unlike us—might have felt and thought in those times."

—MERRILL JOAN GERBER,
author of *The Hysterectomy Waltz* and
*The Kingdom of Brooklyn*

"Lemberger deepens our understanding of the stories we have heard many times and thought we knew. The women of the Bible come alive in all of their vulnerability and power. The stories in this book are a work of modern midrash— so necessary and so beautifully done. Bravo, Michal Lemberger, and may your stories inspire many more."

—RABBI SUSAN GOLDBERG,
Wilshire Boulevard Temple

"Lemberger's stories are marvelous compounds of scholarship, imagination, and empathy. Brought to life with rich historical detail, these biblical women, sidelined and silenced for centuries, prove to be audacious, utterly relatable, and spellbinding companions."

—MICHELLE HUNEVEN,
author of *Blame* and *Off Course*

"Imaginative leaps, the stories in *After Abel* transport the reader into fully realized biblical landscapes where we discover the experiences of characters whose shadowy presence in Hebrew scriptures inspire Lemberger's creative speculation. Like the classical midrashist, she elaborates the spaces between the text's choices, and by giving fullness of life to female presences merely hinted at in the Bible, she participates in the contemporary enterprise of bringing gender balance to the world of our mythic origins."

—LORI LEFKOVITZ,
Ruderman Professor of Jewish Studies,
Northeastern University

"These short stories about biblical women are moving, often ingenious, and even gripping. Lemberger combines an insightful knowledge of biblical women and their stories with an acute ability to more fully imagine their lives in ways that feel true to the biblical text. She answers many of the questions readers have long wanted to know. What did Lot's wife think about her husband's plan to offer his daughters to the men of Sodom? What about Haman's wife? Lemberger writes extremely well, with a touch of humor and plenty of compassion. This is a great read and the perfect choice for book groups and sisterhoods of all sorts."

—ADRIANE LEVEEN, Senior Lecturer
in Hebrew Bible at Hebrew Union College–
Jewish Institute of Religion and author of
*Memory and Tradition in the Book of Numbers*

"A gorgeous book of inspired reimaginings, full of heartbreak and courage and piercing beauty."

—BEN LOORY, author of
*Stories for Nighttime and Some for the Day*

"With a delightful play of the imagination, Lemberger has brought to life biblical characters and episodes that the Bible authors never dreamed of, while remaining gracefully faithful to the cultural 'atmosphere' of biblical times."

—OSCAR MANDEL, California Institute of
Technology Professor Emeritus of Literature
and author of *Otherwise Fables*

"The Hebrew Bible tells only the outline of most of its stories, and over the centuries many have filled in the white spaces with their own notions of back stories and behind-the-scenes drama. Yet rarely have those voices included those of women. In Lemberger's book, these blank spaces are filled in by the stories of women: brave, frightened, loving, and taking extreme measures to protect their children. The women are real, their stories are heartbreaking, their courage undeniable. *After Abel and Other Stories* is a truly welcome addition to understanding what the Bible could mean by looking at a side of the story rarely considered: the story of women."

—TAMMI J. SCHNEIDER, Professor of Religion and
Dean of the School of Arts and Humanities at
Claremont Graduate University and author of
*An Introduction to Ancient Mesopotamian Religion*

# AFTER ABEL

*and other stories*

MICHAL LEMBERGER

With a foreword by Jonathan Kirsch

PROSPECT
· PARK ·
BOOKS

Published by Prospect Park Books
2359 Lincoln Avenue
Altadena, CA 91001
www.prospectparkbooks.com

PROSPECT
· PARK ·
BOOKS

Distributed by Consortium Book Sales & Distribution
www.cbsd.com

**Library of Congress Cataloging-in-Publication Data**
Lemberger, Michal.
 [Short stories. Selections]
 After Abel & other stories / Michal Lemberger ; foreword by Jonathan Kirsch. -- First edition.
    pages cm
 ISBN 978-1-938849-47-3 (alk. paper)
 1. Women in the Bible--Fiction.  I. Title. II. Title: After Abel and other stories.
 PS3612.E454A6 2015
 813'.6--dc23
                          2014041274

Cover design by David Ter-Avanesyan.
Book layout and design by Amy Inouye, Future Studio.
Printed in the United States of America.

*For Anina and Lula*

In men's stories her life ended with his loss.
She stiffened under the storm of his wings to a glassy shape,
stricken and mysterious and immortal. But the fact is,
she was not, for such an ending, abstract enough.

—Mona Van Duyn, "Leda"

# AFTER ABEL

*and other stories*

# CONTENTS

# FOREWORD

The Bible may not be the oldest artifact of the human imagination, but it is the starting point for three world religions and, perhaps even more impressively, a work of authorship that still casts its long shadow across our global civilization. That's why the stories of the Bible have inspired men and women to engage in daring acts of reinvention, a tradition that begins within the pages of the Bible itself, where later-added texts put a new spin on older ones, and continues across the last several millennia. In that sense, *The Alphabet of Ben Sira*, a medieval collection of sometimes-bawdy Bible stories, and *God Knows*, a modern novel styled as the autobiography of King David as reimagined by Joseph Heller, are all examples of the same phenomenon.

And so is *After Abel and Other Stories* by Michal Lemberger. She comes to the Bible honestly, by which I mean that she is willing and able to penetrate the veil of piety that conceals some of its most fascinating and consequential secrets, and she has mastered the intricacies of biblical scholarship that allow us to understand when, why and by whom the Bible was written in the first place. Above all, she is able to enter and inhabit characters who exist for us today only as stray lines of text in the Bible, and she allows us to see the biblical landscape through their eyes.

Lemberger sets herself a lofty goal: "I imagined myself into characters and situations that are well known by dint of being in the most popular book ever published," she explains, "but from an angle that, I suspect, most have never considered." Her exercise in empathy is more than a literary conceit; it can be understood as a reverential act that honors one of the core values of the Bible: "You know the heart of the stranger, for you were once strangers in the land of Egypt." (Exod. 23:9). But it is also a courageous effort to crack open the ancient text and allow the reader to glimpse new meanings in the ancient scriptures.

From the first page of her narrative, and throughout the nine stories collected here, we hear voices that originate in the pages of the Bible and yet, at the same time, ring with passion and candor that is the handiwork of the author. She starts each story with a spare line of biblical text and draws from it a marvelous vision of real people in a real world, and she spins her stories with such conviction and audacity that they come fully alive.

"This won't make it into the official telling," Eve confides to the reader. "The men who will come later to write it all down will leave this part out. Something always gets left out." The Bible tells us that Adam named all of the animals, but it is Eve, in Lemberger's telling, who names the parts of the human body: "Shoulder, elbow, nipple, stomach, shaft, scrotum."

*After Abel* also belongs in another and more recent biblical tradition. Women have been (and still are) excluded from the study and teaching of the sacred texts in certain circles of all three Bible-based religions. Lemberger, however, is to be counted among the women who assert the right to engage in the work of biblical scholarship and have distinguished themselves by their achievements. It is no accident that Lemberger has chosen the most intriguing women of the Bible to write about, some of them deeply familiar—Lot's wife, Miriam, Hagar—and some, like Zeresh, wife of Haman, who have been almost entirely overlooked. Each woman in *After Abel*, however, is depicted with a narrative richness that is mostly lacking in the Bible. The Bible repeatedly shows us that men are privileged to talk to God, for instance, but in Lemberger's stories, women enjoy the same opportunity and exercise it in defiant ways. "You won't trick me again," Hagar says to

God or his emissary. "I know your ways now."

Like the best examples of modern *midrash*, Lemberger's stories can and should be read in conjunction with the passages of the Bible from which they grew and flowered. I suspect, as the author surely intended, that the comparison between the sparse biblical text and Lemberger's lush narratives make a point about how women were regarded by the original authors and editors of the Bible. She has liberated these remarkable women from the constraints imposed on them by the priestly custodians of the sacred text, and she has given them a new birth as figures of flesh and blood, heart and brain.

— *Jonathan Kirsch*

Jonathan Kirsch is the book editor of the *Jewish Journal*, a long-time book reviewer for the *Los Angeles Times*, a guest commentator for the NPR stations in Southern California, and an adjunct professor in New York University's Professional Publishing Program. He is the author of thirteen books, including the best-selling *The Harlot by the Side of the Road: Forbidden Tales of the Bible*.

# AFTER ABEL

*"Adam knew his wife, again, and she bore a son*
*and named him Seth, meaning,*
*'God has provided me with another offspring*
*in place of Abel,' for Cain had killed him."*
Genesis 4:25

———— ◆ ————

This won't make it into the official telling. The men who will come later to write it all down will leave this part out. Something always gets left out.

For so many years, it was just the two of us, and only God to talk to. He's great and powerful, but He doesn't have much to say. He talked enough to set this whole world spinning, but after that, shut His mouth. Now He parcels out His speech: a sentence here, question

there, and short commands in between. And then
Adam, trying his hardest to imitate Him, thinking he's
like God because he guards his words, as if exhausted
by all that naming he did before I came along. It leaves
a woman lonely.

My first boy, Cain, his feet too soft for the hard
earth at first, looked to his father for guidance. I
thought his early babbles meant a change, but then he
fell silent too, hoarded his words as if they were too
precious to share. Only Abel, child of my heart, would
fill the long nighttime hours with stories and songs. His
voice was not pleasing, but it was a sound in this great
empty world.

Adam and I had to figure it all out ourselves, how
our bodies fit together, what they were capable of. We
got better over time, found a private language our bodies
could speak, but in those early days of fumbling, it was all
buck and roll over. Not much in it for me, to be honest.
He thinks he has it so bad, all that work in the fields,
but I'm right there beside him, sowing and harvesting,
breaking my own back to get us fed. He never almost
died from his labor the way I did the second time.

Another thing that won't make it into the final
telling, I'm sure, is the way his labor can lay a man out at
the end of a hard day's work, irritable and hungry if the
fields don't give, the goats run away, but when I labored
to give birth to Abel I bled so badly God Himself had

to step in. That was my first witnessed miracle. If He hadn't saved me, there'd be no more humans. No one around to feed the two babies I'd already birthed, either. No one to replace that one with this new one.

Finally I've figured out how to put them to my breast. It's only now, with Seth, that I've learned how to lift him without the bruising or swellings that hardened under my skin in the months after Cain and Abel were born. He bumps his head against me, mouth open and searching. He lays his hand against my skin as he suckles, smiles up at me, his mouth stretched around my nipple, sighs in pleasure. But it took losing Abel to learn it, and here's me with no girls to teach it to. Just these boys, full of jealousy, and murderous. One dead, the other gone. Where to, I have no idea. We found the body in a field, his head bashed in, face and neck covered in blood already turning to brown, and his brother disappeared. I lost two in one moment, and I felt a gash open in my stomach at the sight of that boy, whom I had brought into the world at the cost, almost, of my own life.

Who was there to teach me what a mother feels when she loses a son? Not God. He'd retreated somewhere beyond our vision. Not Adam, who clasped his hands together, looked down at the ground, and then spent the night with his back turned to me.

When we first found him, I thought he would get back up, his skull would undent, and we four would go back to how we'd been, growing and tending to the land and animals. I think now that Adam understood at once, but it took me longer to recognize or admit to that fly-covered finality.

It's not that I hadn't seen death. Animals died around us all the time. Mauled, torn apart by predators. Some fell sick or got old and curled up under bushes to depart in peace. One bad winter, we lost almost all the lambs. Adam took those deaths so personally at first, each a brief disappointment. Maybe it hardened him, crushed his first impulse to label, to name each creature as it came before him. Which is why it was left to me to find the right names for my sons.

I didn't make the connection between that body lying twisted on the ground and our own brief lives. I thought people lived by a different set of rules. God spoke to us, after all, even if less and less often as time wore on. Surely that made us special. Surely that meant we'd live forever. Scraped, bruised, broken, yes, but we lived. Adam never lost his limp after a fall off a rock shelf on our travels east out of the Garden, but it didn't kill him. It barely slowed him down. That very night he mounted me with an intensity I had never seen in him before. Not a year passed, and I got rounder and rounder, with rumblings under my heart and God mum on what was happening or why.

There too, I had the lesson of the animals to thank,

how they also got fat and then lay down to push out
their young. So I watched and learned. And Cain was an
easy birth, slipped out of me like a gift. Now, two hard
births later, I know what a mercy that was, how God
took pity on me. Or maybe He just fooled me, wanted
to show me how carefully I should have attended to His
words. At the time, though, I thought—but didn't say, I
never said it out loud—that God must have been trying
to scare me with His talk of difficult childbirth.

That first time, a little panting, some cramps, and
then him, slick and covered in white, his face puffy,
but his form a perfect replica of his father's. It seemed
a wondrous connection—the beauty of Adam's body
making this new thing with me. I was fooled by it, fooled
into wanting more, my desire growing stronger as the
weeks and then months passed. It was just as God had
promised, though I didn't pay close enough attention.
My desire was for my husband. I was so young, my body
alive to its tiniest sensations. I wanted Adam again and
again. After we fled the Garden, wrapped in the skins
God had covered us with, we found out what cold was
and clung to one another. But the warmth between
our bodies made Adam's clothes bulge and his breath
quicken. His weight on me, the rocking of his body
into mine, made me crave more. Dark came so early
in those days. Nights I spent cataloging every part of
him, naming and touching—shoulder, elbow, nipple,

stomach, shaft, scrotum. Each a discovery, a new source of delight.

I think now that God must have known how little His words meant to me when He first said them. He must have waited to show me how wrong I had been. He had promised labor, that I would work to bring life into the world. How else to explain the screaming pain of Abel's birth? The pushing and pushing down through my bowels and him not coming, stuck as if in a vessel stoppered with rags. My womb was a cave hiding the clay of his new body from the winds, and it did not want to give him up. Perhaps my body knew, even then, that losing him would be the greater pain.

No, this will not make it into the final account. The men who will come to tell this story will never know that teaching this new baby how to be a man is the important part. They will think the tests ended where punishment began.

I will protect Seth. And he'll be my last. I won't do it again, give over everything in me to make him, only to see him crumbled like a leaf off the tree, the ground mulching to reclaim him.

God didn't tell the whole truth. But I've grown used to that. My desire has changed. It's not for Adam, who continues to reap and plant, reap and plant, whose body grows leaner, his skin slacker, each year. When he turns to me now, I turn away. Everything I have is saved for

Seth, the last of my womb, who has to grow tall, who has to learn better how to survive this world. I have so much to teach him. He needs to know how to speak to God and the world in the languages they understand.

Adam also got it wrong. He focused on the penalties, the pronouncements, on our banishment. But he confused the consequences for the cause. Here's what happened: God said one thing. The snake said another. Which is how I learned that someone had to be lying. That was the knowledge. That was my first step out of the Garden, and no one chasing me with a flaming sword. It wasn't the bite into the fruit or sharing it with Adam. I knew that one of them had told the truth, the other hadn't, and the only way I'd know which was to take the fruit into my hand, into my mouth.

Here is the real lesson. Only God got to say which was good, which bad. Not because of truth. No. He got to decide because we—I—had tasted what it meant to see a future of our own making. That's what He couldn't allow. So He showed us the cost of choosing the wrong truth. Showed us the door and then shut His mouth tight.

Believe me, they're going to get it wrong when they tell my story. They'll miss what it meant to raise my boys. They'll write them off with a sentence. They won't show the mistakes I made, who had no mother to teach me how to love. No father to brush the hair from my face, the dirt from my scrapes. God was our only model, and we took all the wrong lessons: Adam to walk silently through his life, and me, with my decrees and a quick slap across the face when they were defied.

It took this—one dead, the other disappeared—to see what I could not have known all along. Cain was too much like me, too quick to anger, too quick to hide. I have finally learned. I will do better this time. I won't raise my hand. There is no lesson so urgent it has to end with Seth's cheek bruised and streaked with tears. I never want to see a son of mine cower in fear or hide from my anger. That's my promise, even though no one will ever know it.

None of that will replace my other boy though. It won't restore either of them. I was born twice before, once when I woke next to Adam in the Garden's shade, the green world opening to welcome me, the last of its fruits. Then again with that first rush of water between my legs, the small body cradled to my skin. This is the third time, and the last. I cannot be as I was. Adam named me mother of all the living. Now, mother and mourner both, I finally understand. To be mother of the living is also to be mother to all the dead.

Abel, my son, has come and gone, and I, the ground from which he rose, remain.

They won't write it down. They won't know. But I will not forget.

# LOT'S WIFE

*"So Lot went out to them to the entrance,*
*shut the door behind him, and said, 'I beg you, my*
*friends, do not commit such a wrong.*
*Look, I have two daughters who have not known*
*a man. Let me bring them out to you, and you*
*may do to them as you please; but do not do*
*anything to these men, since they have come under*
*the shelter of my roof.'"*
Genesis 19:6-8

————— ◆ —————

S he sat in the small patch of shade, churning the
camel's milk to butter. The courtyard was quiet
with work, one daughter at the oven baking
bread, the other grinding down flour for tomorrow's

loaves. It was good to have these girls, who had learned their way and were of use to those around them.

Slowly, the butter started to come. They'd have it tonight, she thought, along with the bread her daughter was baking, some dates, and a skin of wine.

Good, clean food, but she would admit to counting down the time to the next feast day, when they'd offer up a sheep, a ram if the year continued as well as it had been going, the smell of the meat roasting, the smoke going up to God, the meat going to them. All the hired men would get theirs, she'd make sure of it. Even the slave girls. The family would eat well. She let her mind wander, already preparing the juiciest parts in her mind: crushed figs to bring out the meat's succulence, and cloves for pungency.

These were the moments she cherished. Everyone with her task to do. She could slip into her thoughts instead of keeping her eyes and ears open, alert to what could, and probably would, go wrong. Which is why she didn't hear anything until the voices came closer, until they were in her house. Someone was inside. She glanced at the sky. Sunset wouldn't come for hours. The men were still in the fields, girls in the orchards. But there was no doubt. Voices came through the building. All male. The only one she recognized was her husband's.

She heard him come through the house. He ducked out of the doorway and straightened in the air of the courtyard, near the oven where their daughter was shaping dough into balls.

"We have visitors," he announced. "Traders on their way to Ur. They approached me near the western pastureland."

"Did you take their animals?" she asked without stopping the movement of her arm.

"They had ten altogether. I had to split them up. They've all been watered and fed. Two of the boys are keeping watch over them. But the men brought a few of their bags with them."

"They must have something valuable to sell. Did they offer to show you?"

"No. And I wouldn't ask to see the inside of a man's saddlebags. But these are important men. We have to treat them well. I've told one of the field hands to bring a goat in. Kill it and dress it. We'll need a full meal by tonight."

He turned to go back into the house. "Bring a bowl of water," he ordered his older daughter. "Let the men wash themselves while the meal is being prepared."

She had already begun lighting a fire in the pit at the center of the courtyard when the field hand came in with the animal. He's picked a plump one, she thought.

Soon her older daughter returned, too. "Who are these men, Mama?" the younger one wanted to know.

"I don't know, but they're not from here. Their hair

is curled and uncovered," said the older one.

"They must come from far away," their mother said. "There are places in the world, places you two will never see, where even the men leave their heads bare."

The younger girl continued to bake their bread, adding seeds and saffron to the plain pita they normally ate. The older one took over at the churn, turning the goatskin over and over.

Meanwhile, their mother took the animal to the corner of the courtyard, slit its throat, hung it upside down to drain, and directed the boy to peel off its skin. Once that was done, she quartered and pounded it so that it would grill quickly and still maintain its tenderness. She spread red lentils across the ground, ran her hands and eyes over them, picked out the tiny stones that would try to masquerade themselves in the pot and ruin the dish.

The courtyard rustled with activity. It smelled of death and fire, cumin and bread. These are the scents, she thought as she gathered the picked-over beans and poured them into a large pot, of a good life.

————— ◆ —————

Everyone moved quickly, the time for slow and private thought replaced with a sense of urgency. She looked at her youngest daughters, fourteen and fifteen, and

thought, they are ready to be married. She was determined to keep them closer than the others. She hoped
her husband wouldn't insist on selling them off to the
highest bidders as he had her older girls, though he'd
found good husbands for them. She had to hand him
that. Surely, he'd leave these to their mother. Her old
age was coming. She could feel it in the creases of her
knees and shoulders. She needed her daughters.

It's true they were already older than she had been,
married off at twelve, given over to a much older man
by her father, no say in her own fate, and taken away to
another land.

But Lot hadn't turned out to be a bad husband.
Easily swayed by other men's ideas, and he wouldn't
so much as carry a bucket of milk for her. That was
beneath him. He'd only busy himself with the owning
and bossing. He left all the working to the hired hands.
And to her, of course. But he had a rich and generous
uncle who gave him enough livestock to start his own
herd. And for all his faults, he really wasn't too bad in
business. Mostly, he'd taken her away from the tents,
wandering the desert behind her father's goats. At least
they lived in the city. A real house to sleep and wake in.
Women to sit with in the square at shearing time. Not
like in her youth, when it was just her mother, sisters,
one or two slave girls, and her. And she'd given him
nine live births. Only one son lived to see his maturity,

but the four girls who made it past childhood were of
hardier stock.

And true, she had once had another name. Her
own mother had called her Puha, but she'd been Lot's
wife for so long she had almost forgotten the name of
her youth. Even Lot called her that. But he would, just
as his son was always "son," and his daughters, when
referred to at all, were "Lot's daughters," though she
had named them each as they came into this world, and
named each of the four again as she buried them.

But she wasn't complaining. She had this courtyard
of her own, with its round stove and barrel of flour. It
was more than most had. More than she ever expected
in her youth, when sand crawled into every corner of the
tent and slitted up into her nose and eyes. Now she was
the wife of one of the wealthiest men in Sodom. A third
of the people worked for him. There were only three
other rich families in the town who employed everyone
else. Not that it made a difference to the women. Wives
were wives. The weight of a man's body didn't change
with his wealth.

It would be another hot night. They would all sleep
on the roofs to avoid the stifling rooms below. After the
heavy meal the family and its guests were about to eat,
they'd all crave the cool air, and she had remembered
to replenish the hay pile up there in the morning. The
girls could sleep on the hay. Its smell would fill the air

between them and the stars above.

From up there, she would be able to see all the warrens and ways of the city below. All the houses of her neighbors, and beyond them, the city wall and the land that spread in every direction, some of it theirs, with wheat and barley growing, and a vineyard that always seemed to give grapes in their season.

Too bad we aren't preparing for a real feast, she thought. They hadn't had one since mid-winter, when the whole town had set up altars at the city gates, thanked God for their bounty and banished the dark with song. They were in need of a feast, something to bring everyone together again, especially after the last few months of infighting. Rich men are not to be trusted, she knew. A poor man might steal a donkey or a goat. But a rich man will start a war to claim an entire herd. It was even worse when neighbors fought, when you had to see each other every morning going out through the gate and every night coming back in.

But Lot had gotten through these arguments before. This time it was Pildash, who already had a bigger flock and more pasture than anyone else in Sodom, Lot included. He claimed Lot had cheated him, taken the best pastureland for himself. It was all nonsense. This was the downside of settled life. The nomads of her past never argued like this. They just picked up and moved on when the grass grew thin. Of course, she remembered hearing stories of massacres along the way. There were a few times her father had packed up camp in the middle of the night, the smell of blood still on him.

They all had to live here together, though, so no one would be killing anyone over the pastureland. They'd argue, and someone would slip some coins to the other, and that would be that. And if they couldn't settle it, they'd wait for the judge to make it back to Sodom as he traveled the cities of the plain to decide for them. It would all be taken care of. More civilized, she supposed, but what did she know of that, daughter of a nomad that she still was.

———— ♦ ————

The men had just settled down to eat. Her daughters were still in the courtyard, turning the goat meat one last time before she would bring it inside. In the meantime, her husband and their guests had wine, bread, cheese, and newly picked grapes. She could be proud of her table, and her husband could be counted a generous host. It was then, while the three men were enjoying the bounty of her hands, that the shouting started. At first, it sounded muffled, as if coming from far off, but soon it got louder, and then someone banged on the door.

"Bring them out here. Let us see these strangers you

have taken into your home," one cried out. Then another jeered, "Bring them out so we can get to know them."

A howl of laughter went up from the crowd. It was hard to tell from inside, but she estimated that there were fifteen to twenty men out there. She recognized some of the voices. Men with grudges against Lot, or else the poor of the town who resented his wealth. But why were they getting so riled up? It couldn't really be over a couple of strangers passing through town, she thought. Strangers came through Sodom all the time on the road between market towns. There had to be more to this.

She hurried up to the roof and peeked over the edge. The men below were drunk. Very drunk. That much was clear, and one man was egging the others on. Usually, the other wealthy men in the town could be counted as Lot's closest friends and his only peers. But here was Pildash shouting encouragement to the rest of the crowd. So this is how he'll get what he wants, she thought. He'll embarrass my husband in front of the entire city and these strangers to whom he's offered his hospitality. It was vile behavior, but he knew Lot well. Make him look bad enough and he just might give up that pastureland without too much of a fight. Rich men and their pride, she thought.

No one noticed her up there. They wouldn't see her even if they had looked up, which they wouldn't, because life happened horizontally in Sodom—everyone on the ground, paying attention to the business at hand, except on nights like tonight, when they'd all sleep on the roofs above. All on an even plane. That's the way they liked it here, everyone visible to everyone else. It meant nothing, of course. Four men still paid everyone else's wages. But if you can see them sleep and wake it's easy to overlook how much more they have than you ever will. It had always been this way, the landowners and the shovelers of shit all living side by side, managing to get along.

No one would pay attention to a woman on a roof anyway. She became invisible when men got together in groups larger than three or four. Which was fine with her. So no one saw her as she watched Lot open their door and step out into the hostility and the evening.

"Friends, what can I do for you tonight?" he asked, as if he hadn't heard their demands or their anger.

"Give us the strangers! We haven't met them yet." The men called out of the crowd, one's words overlapping another's. "Who are they? What do they want? Where are their donkeys or camels? What are they trading?"

Everyone was shouting at once and shoving closer and closer to the wall of the house. Lot tried to speak, but they cut him off. Soon, the men were poking him in the chest. Some looked feral, about to attack. All this over some pastureland, she thought, and felt a small twinge of worry. She'd never seen an argument come to this before. She pushed the thought out of her mind. Her husband would work it out, and they'd all go back to their dinners.

But she watched as Lot grew more scared. He pushed back at the men and raised his voice to be heard.

"Friends. You have known me for many years. You know that I deal honestly."

A derisive laugh went up from one or two of the men, but Lot ignored them. "These men are on the road to Ur," he added.

"What are they paying you?" one voice called out of the crowd.

"Yeah! How much are you getting to host these men?"

"We are all citizens here," another called out. "We should all get a share of their bounty."

Finally, Pildash spoke. Unlike the others, he didn't raise his voice. And he wasn't drunk. "Why should you be the only one to get the honor of hosting them? Bring them out here to us. Let's see how tights their assholes are."

Another ugly howl rose from the mass of men. She could smell the stink of them from up here. Lot continued as if no one had spoken, but he raised his voice a little higher, his fear audible at its edges. "They had heard of me from my associates in the west and so

sought me out. I have offered them a meal and a bed
for the night. That is all. They will be on their way in
the morning."

It wasn't working. She could see that. The men were
just getting more and more worked up. From above, she
heard the door slam as Lot rushed back in. She ran back
down and into the house to find him flustered, his cloak
ripped at the neck where someone had grabbed him.

"I have to do something," he said to her. "They'll
break into our house and drag these poor men into the
street."

"They're a drunk mob, she replied. "Throw them
some coins and they'll be happy."

"You heard them. They want the men."

"They want money."

"They'll do unnatural things to those men. I cannot let my guests be raped by a bunch of drunken
farmhands."

"Don't be ridiculous. They don't want to do them
any harm," she said, with as much vehemence as she
dared. Her husband could be irritatingly literal sometimes, but woe to her if she pointed that out. She had
long ago learned to soothe his pride if she wanted to
get anywhere. "They want to shake them down. Someone saw the men's bulging saddlebags. Now they think
they're rich, that they should pay some sort of tax to be
allowed to stay here for the night."

"They're my guests! I must protect them," he insisted. "The men outside are out of control."

"Then go out with a few skins of wine as a peace offering, compliments of the visitors."

"You're not listening to me, woman! Didn't you hear them? What do you think 'let us see how tight their assholes are' means?"

"It means they want to see if they have any gold hidden under their clothes! Come on," she added, forcing her voice to be as soothing as possible. "These are our neighbors. You know them. They're as corrupt as the next person, but what you're suggesting is truly unthinkable."

But Lot wasn't listening to her. He was pacing, his head bent in concentration.

Finally he lifted his head. "Go get the girls," he said.

"The girls?"

"My daughters. Go get them."

"Why?" she said, no longer trying to hide her alarm. "What are you going to do with them? What do they have to do with this?"

"They'll take the girls instead."

"You're going to throw our children to that mob? Are you crazy?"

Finally, he looked at her, but it was as if they'd never met before, much less buried four children together. "I have no choice. Our family's honor is on the line."

Fully hysterical now, she cried out, "Honor! Those men will kill our girls. They will rip them apart from the inside and leave them for dead. How much honor can you have if you are willing to let that happen to your own children?"

"You heard those men! They will do that to my guests! Besides, you're the one who said they wouldn't rape anyone."

"I said they wouldn't rape the travelers. But they have money. They can pay off those drunks and everything will die down. You'll go back to your dinner and this will all be forgotten by morning. But our girls have nothing but their bodies. They have nothing else to offer. If, by some miracle, they manage to survive what twenty grown men can do to them, we'll never be able to marry them to anyone. You'll ruin them forever. Or kill them first."

She was still coherent, but in tears and clawing at her husband's clothing. But Lot had heard enough.

"Get them! Now!" He turned back and opened the door again to face the crowd. She could only hear the first few words out of his mouth—"Friends! I've come make you an offer"—before the door closed behind him.

———— ◆ ————

Before she could move, before a thought could form in her mind, a well of anger rose from her stomach into her throat. In an instant, he went from her husband, the man who had brought her into his home and bed so many years before, to a viperous stranger. She would fight him, to the moment of her own death, if she had to. He won't take them, she thought. That monster won't take them from me.

She only had a few minutes. She ran back to the courtyard, grabbed whatever she could—tufts of goat skin, batches of raw wool left over from the recent shearing, and a pot of oil still cooling next to the fire. All the while, she shouted to the girls, "Run up to the roof. Now. As fast as you can. Grab whatever valuables you see on your way. Silver plates, gold coins, jewelry. Anything."

They were slow to move, began asking questions, "Why, Mama?"

"Not now!" she screamed. "Just run."

She stuffed the wool into a piece of still-bloody goatskin, grabbed an unlit torch from the ground and thrust it into the oven, waited for the loud whoosh as its end caught. Then she hurried up to the roof. Her daughters soon followed, each carrying a saddlebag bulging with small objects. She had no time to inspect what they'd taken. She was already putting the torch to the pile of hay in the corner.

"Mama!" they cried. "What are you doing? We'll burn up!"

"No, we won't, we'll be long gone by the time this is big enough to harm us."

From below, she could hear her husband trying to speak over the noise of the angry crowd. Slowly, slower than she could stand, a wisp of smoke rose from the hay pile. Once it did, she started grabbing tufts of wool out of the skin she had brought up and shoved them at her children. "Start lighting them," she directed.

Confused and scared, the girls did as they were told and dipped each piece into the pot of oil. Their mother hopped from their roof to the neighbor's, grabbing a flaming ball of wool as she did, hurling it down into the narrow street in front of her house. The girls followed her, handing her their fiery missiles as they moved. They went from rooftop to rooftop, setting each hay pile on fire and throwing more projectiles down to the city below.

"Mama," panted the younger girl, "what are we doing? They'll kill us when they realize what we've done."

"They won't see us," she said. "They can't see us over the lip of the roof. And anyway, by the time anyone below thinks to look up, we'll already be on another one."

"But what are we trying to do?" cried the older girl. "And why? I don't understand."

"I'm saving you," was the only answer her mother would give.

From below, they could hear screaming as people all around the cramped city began to notice that their streets and homes were on fire. The worst of it, they saw, was concentrated near Lot's house, where a few men had been hit directly and were trying desperately to put themselves out. They rolled on the ground, screaming in fear and pain, but it was too late for them. Their neighbors watched as they were consumed in flames.

"Help!" came the people's desperate cry. "What vengeance is this? Why does God rain down fire on us?"

Panic spread as people rushed to save their own homes, pushing others down, trampling them if they had to. By then, she and her daughters had reached the roof of the farthest home, where the poorest inhabitant of the city lived, an old widow with no family to care for her. Dependent on begging and whatever she could gather to sell in the market, the widow lived in a small house set into a narrow patch of the city wall.

The three women had to hop down to reach its roof, which had no hay pile and nowhere to sleep on hot summer nights. She was sure her daughters could jump down from there to the ground, but her own old body was already feeling the effects of the run across the city's rooftops. I've come this far, she thought. Just see them to safety. They are all that matters.

Standing at the lip of the house, they could hear the screams coming from all over Sodom. The fire had spread farther than she could have imagined, "Quick," she told her daughters, "throw away the wool," and she flung the still-burning torch as far as she could. "Now, jump," she said, practically pushing them off the roof. As soon as they were off, she followed, landing hard on one ankle, but she didn't stop to think about it.

Once on the ground, she banged on the door. "Open up," she shouted. "We have to escape!"

The old woman inside shuffled to the door.

"The city is on fire," she said. "We'll help you out the window, but we must be quick." The three younger women pulled the old lady to the far end of her tiny house. Through the window they could see the plain stretching as far as the shimmering lake and the distant hills beyond it. They lifted her out and set her down onto the ground outside the city walls, then followed her.

"The city is on fire!" she repeated when it became clear the old woman didn't understand what was happening. "Get as far away from it as you can." Then, to her daughters, she shouted, "Run. Head for the lake. Don't stop and don't turn around. There's nothing here for us anymore."

———————◆———————

The girls took off, sprinting like gazelles across the flat land. She followed behind, going as fast as she could, the heat from the blaze growing stronger on her back. Soon, she could barely see her daughters in the distance, just two slender forms moving easily through the night. But her ankle throbbed. Her breasts pounded painfully against her chest with every step, and she struggled to find breath.

"Keep going," she told herself. "Get them to safety. Save your children."

Eventually, she felt the ground change beneath her feet. She had run past fields, her husband's and others'. The earth was harder, paler in the brightening moonlight than the rich soil of the plain. She was getting closer to the lake. They wouldn't be able to stay there, out in the open, even on a warm night like tonight. They'd have to go further, up into the foothills, but she felt safer now that she had run this far.

Up ahead, she could see her daughters, the surface of the water winking behind them as they waited for her to catch up. But she couldn't take another step. She was too tired. Her breath caught with every inhalation. She worked hard every day of her life, but she had not run like this since her own childhood, when there was time for games, when she and her brothers and sisters ran through the flocks, teasing the animals and running away before they could get hurt.

Bending over, her chest heaved painfully. She rested her hands on her soft thighs. Her whole body seemed to be trying to breathe. Even her arms and legs shook from the effort.

Standing back up, she reeled as the blood rushed away from her head, sent her body staggering and turned her to face the way she'd come. The plain stretched out behind her. In the distance, a few small figures scuttled away from Sodom, which was still burning, higher now than she ever thought possible.

Only then, as she watched those tiny human shapes, did the truth of what she had done hit her with its full force. Those were her neighbors, people she had lived among for decades, ever since Lot brought her here, one child on her hip, another in her womb. Images of the life she had led, of her husband and children, passed quickly through her mind. Then others. Her friends. The courtyard she'd claimed as her own. The bed she had shared with one man since the age of twelve. It was all gone. Her husband, who would have whored his own daughters out over some foolish sense of pride, he was in there too, and though her rage still flared hotter than any fire, she felt, in that moment, what it was to lose an entire life, her own history of love and of loss.

For the first time, she saw what her hands had wrought. I have killed, she thought. I have killed and I have destroyed. She had to repeat it aloud a few times before she began to believe it. "I have killed today. I have killed to save my own."

It was only in that moment, when her body struggled to reassert itself and her mind fought to align her pride at having saved her children with her grief at losing everything she still held dear, her whole valued life, and horror at what she had wrought, that she started to cry. Huge, dehydrated tears poured down her face, heaving sobs wracked her body. She shivered, cold sweat mingling with the heat of her long run, and she sank down, crying harder than she ever had cried before, harder even than the morning her own mother had sent her away into her new marriage and the long life ahead of her.

She could see her girls walking toward her, and though she didn't want them to see her cry, didn't want them to doubt what they had done, she couldn't stop. Something had opened within her. Try as she might, she could not close it.

"Stand up, Mama," one of them said. "You have to keep moving or your muscles will seize up."

———◆———

And she would. She would get up. She would let her daughters, each as tall as she was now, half-carry her along the lake's shoreline and up into the hills. She would find a cave for them to stay in for the night, her girls curled around her like lambs, would collapse into an exhausted, grief-stricken sleep. She would wake the next morning to explain to her bewildered children that they could never return to their homes, that they would have to forget all they had ever known, even their father, and look only into the future. She would calm them when the full shock of what they had done hit them, and their fear of God's wrath shook within them. She would explain that they had done God's work the previous night, or the work God should have done when a man would ask a mother to sacrifice her virgin daughters for his own stupid honor. She would tell them they were instruments of God's wrath, that God had guided her hand and theirs when they set their home alight.

And then they would all sleep again. When they next woke, she would drink the water her daughters had collected from a nearby spring and eat the figs they had picked from a tree along the way. She would face their anger when they accused her of ending their lives, of making sure that there would be no man left in the world who would have them. She would soothe them, say that the riches they had stuffed into the saddlebags before they ran from the city would buy them a new life. She would brush off their suspicion that fatherless daughters could achieve anything other than lonely destitution. She would promise to find a way.

Within a few days, once her ankle healed, she would keep that promise, take them to a small market town where no one knew them. She would find an unscrupulous or incurious broker who would take her money and hire a man for her. Her man would go out, purchase land where the three women would live.

At first, he would ask when, as she had promised, his master would arrive. After a while, in the face of her silence, he would stop asking. She would direct him to buy sheep and goats, to hire field hands and shepherds and slave girls. And when they had enough new wealth, she would send the man out again to find husbands for her daughters. She would see them married and grow large with child. She would hold her grandchildren on her lap and know she had done something good. But for all that she would go on to do, Lot's wife, who had once been called Puha, would never rise from that spot by the side of the moonlit lake. She would never stop crying fat, salty tears for the life she left behind in flames.

# DRAWN
# FROM THE WATER

*"A certain man of the house of Levi*
*went and married a Levite woman.*
*The woman conceived and bore a son;*
*and when she saw how beautiful he was,*
*she hid him for three months. When she could hide*
*him no longer, she got a wicker basket*
*for him and caulked it with bitumen and pitch.*
*She put the child into it and placed it*
*among the reeds by the bank of the Nile.*
*And his sister stationed herself at a distance*
*to learn what would befall him."*
Exodus 2:1-4

———◆———

have a special job for you today, Miriam," Amma says.
She woke me even earlier than usual today. Everything
is black, the walls of our hut, the ceiling, and the sky
outside that I can see through the doorway.

It's hard to get out of bed so early. Usually, Baba
is gone by the time Amma rubs my back until I open
my eyes. Not today. Baba is standing right behind
Amma when she wakes me, which is how I know this
is important.

Baba holds up the basket that Amma has been
working on for weeks. First, she sent me to the river
to gather long reeds for her. She cut those up and wove
them together so that I couldn't see through them at all
when I held the basket up to the light. After that, she
carried it down to the river to line it with thick mud.
That sat in our hut drying for days, but it didn't bother
me.

It was different when she started to rub pitch on
the outside. Our hut smelled so bad that I had to hold
my nose every time I walked in. She tried scrubbing
her hands with sand to get the sticky off. She plunged
them into river water. Nothing got it off, which is why
she made me hold the baby for hours. "Don't let him
cry," she told me, so I rocked and made funny faces and
dipped my finger into cane water and let him suck on
it. Amma fed him a lot, too, but it was getting harder
to keep that up.

He's not a bad baby. He squirms around, and he cries. A lot. That's not a problem at night. All the Egyptians go home to their real houses and leave us alone, but during the day they're everywhere, and if they catch anyone hiding a baby boy, they become enraged.

It's always like this when they pass a new law. Right at the beginning they're so strict, and anyone caught breaking the rules gets in big trouble. After a while, though, they relax a bit. Baba says they get bored and look for new ways to torment us, but Amma makes him shush up. She tells him not to talk like that in front of me, because she doesn't want me to repeat those things where an Egyptian can hear me.

Sometimes I talk too much. That's what she says. It makes my Baba laugh, though, when I tell him all the things I see during the day. He doesn't laugh too much, so I've been working really hard to improve my memory so that I can make him happy.

This rule about the babies isn't that old. We all have to be careful. Amma reminds me every day not to say anything if a baby is born in the huts. "I know," I tell her. "I'm already eight years old. I'm not a little girl who doesn't understand anything."

It's pretty bad around here these days. We've all been forced to watch as women who still walk funny from giving birth get pushed to the edge of the river. An overseer pokes her back with the end of his whip and then forces her to throw her own baby into the water. One lady still had blood running all down her legs. That got mixed up with the cuts from the flogging she got right after. The overseers want to make sure that we all know not to try to disobey the Pharaoh's decrees.

I felt really bad for those mothers. They were weeping and shrieking. Baba told me they weren't crying from the beatings. The grown-ups all try not to cry when those things happen, even the men, who are pretty used to seeing people get beat up by now.

"You are the fastest runner, Miriam," Amma says as she takes the basket from Baba and puts it in my hands. It's big and round and heavier than it looks, probably from all the mud and leaves she put inside. Pitch always dries heavier than I expect, too. I peek inside and see the baby in there. That surprises me. So it's not the basket that's heavy, but him, who's all dimpled and fat because Amma feeds him so much. "You'll have to run very quickly to keep up with him."

It's true what she says about me. I am a good runner. I'm faster than all the other kids, even the boys. Baba says it's because my legs are so long. When he wants to tease me, he pinches my calves and says he's helping me develop my muscles. It tickles and hurts at the same time when he does that, which makes me laugh until I can hardly breathe.

"Take him down to the river," she says, "and put him

in somewhere safe. Stay with him. The tide may rush in places, and the wind could blow the water even quicker. Run along the bank. Don't let him out of your sight."

I'm not sure how she thinks this baby is going to survive when so many others haven't, but I don't say anything, because Amma and Baba are looking at me with such serious faces. Sometimes I think Amma must be the wisest woman in Goshen and that she can read my mind, because she takes the baby out of the basket and puts her nose right to his little head. Her mouth is smashed up against him, so I can't hear her too well, but she repeats it for me. "This one is special."

Well, yeah, but all the grown-ups are always telling us that every baby is special, no matter what the Egyptians say. If that's true, then why did some others end up drowning in the Nile?

It's a tricky thing to be a slave. The men have it pretty hard. They have to go out to the fields or building sites when the sky is still half-black and half-orange, and they work until their backs are twisted. I help my Amma pack down the dirt of the floor in our hut every day so Baba can lie down with his knees bent up when he gets back.

By the time they come back at night their shadows are really long. That's a lot of hours to pretend nothing hurts, which they have to do. You never know which overseer is going to decide to make someone do extra work or kick a man he sees scrunch his face up or bend over to stretch. They get cut and scraped all the time, too. The women make buckets of salve to coat their skin, and then use it up in a week and have to make more.

But the women have it worse. My chest is flat and my hips are still skinny. "Nonexistent," my Amma calls them. She says, "You're lucky now, but just you wait." Even I can see the problems older girls face. Girls my age don't get bothered by the overseers, but once they start to look like real women, things get really tricky.

It's like with the babies. If the Pharaoh tells you that you have to drown all your boys as soon as they're born, it would make sense just to stop having babies for a while, at least until the Egyptians lose interest in this latest rule. But that's a not a good solution, because any woman who catches the eye of an overseer can't let him think she's barren. The overseers want to take girls off behind a pile of bricks, but they don't want to have any children with slave women. That would lead to a whole host of trouble for them, and if there's one thing an overseer doesn't want, it's trouble.

Here's how it works. If the baby is a girl, they can pretty much ignore everything and pretend nothing happened. But what if the baby is a boy? That's when the problems begin for him, no matter how long his whip is. He can either claim the baby and try to take him, but the mother and her family will do just about anything to keep a Hebrew baby out of the hands of the Egyptians. They'll hide him, pass him from hut to hut, or pretend he's another woman's child. That could make the overseer angry, which is dangerous.

Overseers are used to getting their way, mostly because they're the ones with the whips in their hands. My Amma says the only way they know how to solve problems is by counting out lashes. If he's admitted that he's the father of a slave woman's child, he can't just walk away and let other people think the Hebrews have tricked him. So he gets angry, which always leads to some of us getting punished. Overseers are really the lowest of the low among the Egyptians, even if they lord it over us. They have bosses, too. If he ruins or even kills any of the slaves he'll be in really big trouble.

That's one option. The other thing he could do is deny that the baby is his. Some of them do that, but it hasn't always worked out so well, because even though the bosses don't really care what the overseers do to the women around here, they don't want to see any more Hebrew babies being born. So they make that overseer personally throw his child in the river. You'd think that would be pretty easy for someone who rejects his own baby, but that's not usually what happens. Amma says only the most hard-hearted man could do that without a stain spreading on his soul.

My friends and I saw one of the meanest overseers

walk into the very same spot in the river where he had to toss in his own son the day before. He was the kind of man who always laughed when a slave clutched his arm or leg in pain and whipped harder than any of the others just because it seemed like fun to him. He wasn't so tough in the end, though. We watched him walk out pretty far into the water. That's when it began to look like he changed his mind about drowning. He waved his hands until he couldn't do that anymore, but we didn't call anyone to save him. None of the Hebrews could do anything to help anyway, since we aren't allowed to learn how to swim. We all stay close to the sides when we go in, and never let the water rise higher than our waists. Some of the bigger boys walk in all the way up to their chests, but that seems like a really bad idea to me. They wouldn't be able to do anything if they fell down. The water would just carry them away and they'd die.

Not one slave cried when his body washed up on the shore.

That's why the women have to stay pregnant, even if it means they might give birth to boys. It's the only way to keep the overseers from following them around, sometimes pushing them down onto the ground right there in the open, but that leaves them back where they started. So they just have to hope for girl babies, or that they'll miscarry or have stillborns. Amma says, "A live birth is a beautiful thing, but not here. It would be better for them not to have lived at all than to be born a slave."

Being pregnant only keeps the women safe in one way. Other than making the overseers keep their dirty hands to themselves, being with child actually makes things harder. The Egyptians call us animals, so they expect the women to squat wherever they happen to be when their time comes and push out a newborn like an antelope or cow does, but we're people, and human women can't really do that, at least most of them.

It's the saddest thing to see a woman who can't even stand up anymore on her hands and knees in the fields, screaming and writhing, but none of us can go help her for more than a second or two at a time for fear of being whipped for stepping away from our own work.

We all find ways to help, though. When we see a woman begin to have her birth pains, all of a sudden the work that day somehow has to be done right where she is. Someone brings her a sip of water when no Egyptian is looking, and the little children who are too young to lift or cut put their warm bodies against her back. It doesn't really do anything, so far as I can see. She'll still moan and thrash around, but afterward those mothers always say that having the children up next to them made the whole thing bearable.

The best thing would be to hide those pains altogether. It's better that the Egyptians just not know when a woman goes into labor. If it does turn out to be a boy, everyone can lie and say it was stillborn, or swap in a newborn girl to carry around in case one of the Egyptians notices that some lady who was waddling around isn't pregnant anymore. In the meantime, we all try to hide the boys.

It's all pretty complicated, but not for me. Because I'm a fast runner, I'm sent on errands instead of having to work in the fields and construction sites. I run between them, delivering messages and things like that. I get to see a lot of things that go on. At night, I pull up all the things I saw that day and tell them to my Amma and Baba. As I said, I have a good memory.

Like the day the decree about the babies was read out. All the men were busy making bricks and hauling them. It was so hot, and I had already been sent all over for hours. The overseers didn't even bother making sure any women were there. They just walked through the site, stopping little groups of men to read off their papyrus and then told them to get back to work. But they couldn't. Not right away. Each little cluster just stood there, as if someone had grabbed hold of their arms and legs and wouldn't let them move.

I don't understand grown-ups. The overseers started hitting people, which is what got the men back to their tasks, but they didn't say anything. They didn't cry or get angry, or anything. The work site got really quiet.

The only sounds were of hammers splitting rock and the wet slap of cement. For the rest of the day, they just kept looking at each other. It was as if they were trying to speak without actually talking. When the men met up with their wives and daughters later that night, it was a totally different story. The women made enough noise to make up for the men's silence. I had to hold my ears closed. It was giving me a headache.

It didn't make any sense. The men didn't say a thing, but then the women shouted or fell down onto the ground. One even screamed at her husband. "It isn't enough that they took our land and our cattle and our dignity. Now they're actually trying to kill us, and you can't even open your mouth."

Her belly was huge, so I guess I can see why she'd be upset, but her husband still didn't say a single word. It was like someone had stolen his tongue. Instead, he rubbed her back, which wasn't going to help anybody once that baby was born.

After that the whispering started. Not right away, but over the next few days. I'd be sent to a field with a message for one of the Egyptians, and a Hebrew woman would call me over, tell me that all the girls and women had come up with an idea, and that I should tell the men to start taking bits of mortar and rock dust home with them at the end of the day.

Then I'd run to the building sites and tell my father

or some other man I knew what the women had told me. They'd nod, and tell me to relay the message that some of the women should start collecting leaves and feathers.

That's how our huts started sprouting hiding places. The men would come home, as tired and broken down as ever, and build little nooks in the corners or off a back wall. And so many women began to look pregnant. Every day, I'd see someone adjusting a lumpy mound as it shifted under her clothes.

The tricks mostly worked. The Egyptians couldn't tell who was really having babies and who wasn't. Even so, they caught a few. Those were really bad days. We all put ashes on our heads. It was the groans that came from the hut where the baby's parents lived that were the worst. I don't know how they did it, because our huts are tiny, but so many women crowded in on those evenings to be with the parents. I couldn't go. Too loud, and anyway, too sad.

And all that time, Amma's belly was getting bigger for real, which made us all very nervous. Even my little brother, who's only five and can be pretty stupid most of the time, started acting even stranger than usual. He wouldn't listen to anyone, and for one whole week pretended he was a crocodile. He wouldn't even eat sitting up, but crawled around sneaking up behind everyone and snapping at their ankles until we'd put his food on the ground. Not in his bowl, but actually pour the food out, even if it was soup.

Of course, Amma and Baba got mad at him, but they also told me that little children act strangely when they can tell something's wrong but don't understand it. I did understand it, because I'm a lot smarter than he is. That's why I got so frightened.

I tried to keep it in, because Amma and Baba were upset enough on their own, but I couldn't do that forever. "What's going to happen?" I finally asked.

Amma looked even more tired than usual. Her skin had gotten kind of grey, like the dust of the rock quarry had been rubbed onto it and stayed there. By then, she was tottering from side to side when she walked, so I knew that the baby would be born soon.

"We'll figure something out," she said.

"But what?"

"I don't know." She sounded tired, too, but she must have done that thing where she read my mind, because she said, "If he's a boy, we'll hide him, just like all the others. But we'll hope for a girl."

But he was a boy. We got lucky, because he was born at night, so the midwives could sneak in and out of the hut without anyone seeing, but Baba told me to go to sleep right after he was born, even though I wasn't tired at all. Amma was crying as she held the baby. Baba, too. I wanted to do something to help, but I couldn't, so I cried too, only I turned my face to the wall so they wouldn't see me.

We did hide him, for a little while, but like I said, he cries a lot, which is bound to call attention to him sooner or later, and that is why there's this basket in my hands now. It's good that I'm so strong, because it's a pretty far walk to the river, and Amma sent me out really early this morning so no one would see me. The baby is staying quiet, probably from all the juggling around as I walk.

I didn't say anything to Amma, but I'm more scared now than ever. What if the basket doesn't float and I have to watch my baby brother drown? What if the tide turns it over and he slips out, or there's a crocodile nearby? Even running as fast as I can, I won't be able to do anything if any of those things happen.

I try to remember what Amma said and repeat it over and over to myself. "We have to have faith. It will turn out okay." I don't know if I believe it, but I believe my Amma.

When I get to the river, I look for a spot along the bank where I can walk in. I think that somewhere with reeds to hide us but also a gentle slide where I won't have to climb down a steep ledge would be best.

The basket is getting even heavier. I don't understand why my arms are trembling. I'm not cold at all. Actually, I'm covered in sweat. By the time I find the perfect spot,

I almost can't hold it up anymore.

The water feels so good. It's cold, but I was so hot that it feels really nice to walk into it. I wade in a little bit, hugging the basket the whole time. I'm afraid it will float away before I'm ready, so I don't want to go too far away from the bank.

It really is too heavy for me, so I have to put it down. I hold onto it with my hand as I back up until the water only covers my ankles and then my feet. It's pretty uncomfortable to be bent over so far, my feet in the shallow end, my arm stretched all the way out so that the basket doesn't float away.

At the last minute, I pull it back in and unlatch the top to look at my brother. "I may never see you again," I say. He just looks up at me. He has one foot in his mouth, which is what he likes to do when he's lying down. It's pretty funny-looking and usually makes me laugh, but not today. Then I get worried that he understood me and will get scared once I let him go, so I say, "Don't worry, I'll be next to you the whole time." I hope that's the truth.

Eventually, I have to let go. At first, the basket doesn't move much. It just bobs up and down on the water and turns around in the reeds. I worry that I chose a bad spot, and that he'll just stay stuck there forever. I don't even know what to do. My chest feels tight and I'm not breathing quite right. But I can't walk into the

water to free the basket, because then I'll be stuck in the
same situation I was afraid of to begin with.

I can't make up my mind. Now we're both stuck,
the baby in the rushes and me just watching the little
basket. It bumps into some reeds, which turns it so that
it bumps into some more. Thankfully, the river makes
a decision for me, because I see the basket start to edge
out to where the current can take it.

Once it's past the rushes, I start to follow it. The
current must be really comfortable, because the baby
doesn't cry at all. That makes me mad, because he never
stopped crying at home, which was the reason we're
here in the first place.

"Were you trying to get put out here?" I say, even
though I know he can't hear me, and that even if he
could, he wouldn't be able to answer.

The water moves pretty slowly, so I walk along, not
even needing to jog to keep up. It starts to get really
boring. Nothing is happening. The basket doesn't even
get pulled into the middle of the river. It just knocks
along the banks. Some mud has started to stick to the
bottom and sides, which is hard to see because of all
the tar, but I can tell, because it looks bumpier than
before. Amma had been really careful with it. She had
smoothed the pitch out with a giant leaf over and over.
At the time, I didn't understand why, but now I see that
she must have thought the basket would float better

that way.

It doesn't seem to be making a difference. The basket keeps floating along. I walk beside it. It floats. I walk. The sun is out for real now. The baby is probably nice and cool in the basket, but I'm getting hot. Flies keep buzzing around my ears and hair, so I spend a lot of time swatting them away. Now I'm bored and irritated. I start kicking pebbles as I walk. I even bend down to pick a few bigger rocks up so that I can throw them.

I'm really good at throwing, and these rocks fit perfectly in my palm. I stop, point to where I want the rock to land in the water, pull my arm back, and fling it over my head. It lands far out in the river with a splash and sinks right away.

I'm about to throw another one when I look around and see that the basket has floated up ahead of me. My chest tightens up again. I lost track of why I was here. Amma and Baba would be so mad if they saw me. I feel terrible and sprint to catch up. The basket hasn't gone very far, but I drop the rest of the rocks out of my fist anyway. I can't throw them while I'm walking, and I'm afraid I'll fall behind again.

It's a good thing I do catch up, because the current starts to speed up a little. I can see bigger ripples on the surface of the water. The color changes, too. It's always brown and muddy, but it's darker now. The basket picks up speed. I'm loping along beside it now, which is better. Not so boring.

That's when the basket moves away from the bank. I have to run to keep up now. The basket tips from side to side more in the water. I get scared that it will tip so far that the baby will fall out, and then all of my Amma's work will be for nothing. Worse than that, I'll have to go back and tell her what happened, and she'll get mad that I didn't save him even though she knows that I can't swim.

All the rocking must be scary for the baby because he starts to cry. I look around, afraid that someone will hear and figure out that this is a Hebrew baby. Then they'd find me and know for sure. I stand on my tiptoes to look around, but there's nothing to see. The river must have carried the basket, and me, along the shore far enough that we've reached a spot that's completely empty. No houses, no roads, no people. It's pretty here, with lots of trees. Their leaves hang over the ground and water, so I can walk in the shade.

This place doesn't look like it does where we live. It's pretty much always noisy there, because the Egyptians make us live so close together. Practically every hut touches another one. And there are lots of kids running around. That's in the morning and at night. I'm not usually there during the day. Since most people are out working in the fields or building sites, I suppose it gets quiet then, but I've never really thought about it too much.

Here it's different. What's that word my Baba uses when he finally gets a chance to lie back and close his eyes? "Peaceful." That's how it feels here. All I can hear is the water. The birds, too. They talk back and forth to each other from the treetops. Some of them are on branches so skinny I don't understand how they can balance up there.

They start to make a racket soon enough, though. It sounds like clack, clack, clack, and a lot more of them than I thought were around start flying from tree to tree. I'm not sure why they're so nervous and loud, until I hear voices up ahead of me.

Whoever they are, they'll see me really soon. To make matters worse, they're all Egyptians. I don't know what to do. If I keep walking, they'll see me for sure. They could do anything then. I could get a whipping, or be sent far away from my parents if one of them decides to keep me for herself, but the basket is still moving, and Amma told me not to lose sight of it. Even though it's shady, I start to sweat again. I wish my Amma was here with me. She'd know what to do.

I glance over at the basket and see that the current has slowed down again. Thank goodness for that, at least. The water bobs the basket along gently. It's headed for a marshy bit up ahead, which should slow it down even more.

The only thing I can do now is hide and hope those people don't see me or the basket. I spot a clump of reeds a few steps away and I push right into the center of it and then crouch down as far as I can. From there, I can put my eye right up to a space between two green shafts and see what's happening, but no one will be able to see me.

The only problem is that I've lost sight of the basket. I just hope it's hidden, too. "What do I do now, Amma?" But I whisper so softly that she wouldn't be able to hear me even if she was right there beside me. Anyway, I'm old enough to know that she won't be able to answer. It's just that she'd know what to do, and I don't.

The voices get closer. They're laughing while they walk. Then I see them. Three girls, maybe twelve or thirteen years old. At least I think that's how old they are, but they look so different from anyone I've ever seen that it's hard to tell.

They're beautiful. One of them is tall, with long arms. I bet she runs fast, because her legs are long, too. Another one has the kind of rosy, round cheeks that I've never seen on a Hebrew child. It's like her face is trying to laugh even when her mouth isn't. The last is small. She's not much taller than I am, but she already has breasts, which is how I know she's older than I am.

All three of them are wearing gold necklaces that

reach from their necks down to the tops of their chests and wink back at the water. Their eyes look really long across their faces, almost as if they touch where the tops of their noses should be, but then I realize that they just have very dark paint around them. Their hair is blacker than any I've ever seen and perfectly straight, with beads woven into the ends and some kind of wrap around the tops of their heads. Those hairbands are the most amazing of all. They have beads of all different colors strung together to make patterns of fish and eyes and the symbol of the Pharaoh, which is one that all the Hebrews know well, since we have to carve it into so many of the buildings that get put up.

And their clothes. They wear skirts that open in the front to let them walk and shirts that look like they're attached to their necklaces. I want to go up to them and put my hand on the cloth because it looks so clean. It's all white. Really and truly white and not stained with sweat or ripped and sewn back up in places.

I almost don't believe that these girls are real. I'm so caught up in staring at them that I don't follow their eyes. So I jump in surprise when one of them points and says, "What's that over there?" It looks like she's pointing right at me, and the shivering in my arms starts up again, but then I see them walk down to the edge of the water and peer at another bunch of rushes.

They start to talk to each other, and even though I

know Egyptian, their words stumble out on top of each other so quickly that I don't understand what they're saying. What I can see is that they seem nervous. They may even be as scared as I am. It's like they've taken over for the birds and are chattering back and forth to each other in fright.

Someone else must have heard them, too, because I hear her ask, "What now, girls?" Whoever she is she sounds a little frustrated, as if this is how they always act and that it gets tiresome for her to listen to it.

The girls' heads jerk up at the sound of that voice, but they don't say anything. They look at each other, lift their shoulders, and gesture with their hands as if to ask each other what they should do. The voice comes again, "Well, what's there?"

One of the girls finally speaks up. "It's a basket, Mistress. Floating in the water. It sounds like it's crying."

"Baskets don't cry," the voice says. I can't see her, and it's probably true that a person doesn't have to grow up a slave to know that this lady is the boss, but I figure all Hebrew children would know for sure. In any case, I know she's the boss, and that the three girls answer to her and are a bit afraid of her, too.

"Yes, Mistress," the tall girl says, but none of them move.

"Well, don't just stand there. Bring it over to me."

I watch the girls as carefully as I have ever looked

at anything. I'm wondering what they'll do to my baby brother, when I hear the sound of water moving. The girls have already lifted up the hems of their skirts to wade into the water to get the basket, pushed the reeds aside, and lifted it out. Now I can see the basket again. It looks exactly the same as it did before. I follow the girls' eyes. I see a woman rise out of the river.

The others are beautiful, but this one makes my mind go silent. I didn't know people could look like this. The three holding my baby brother's life in their hands are just copies. It's just obvious, even though this one doesn't even have any clothes on.

As she rises, the water falls away from her. She's like a stalk, long and slender. Her whole body is lit up, like the shiniest bronze. There's no hair on her, except for the long black strands that fall over her shoulders and back. I've seen slave women naked millions of times, and none of them looks like this.

I wonder if all Egyptians are like this, as sleek under their clothes as the statues in their temples. But then I remember the overseers. Some of them have thick, curly hair on their arms and chests. And they all have furry legs. That's what makes me think this woman must be special.

I can't take my eyes off of her. It's like she carries a sun around with her, only this one can be looked at without burning my eyes. My Amma always told me

that the Egyptians are no better than us, even if they
tell us they are all the time. Amma knows just about
everything. I almost can't believe that she's wrong, but
I've never seen a Hebrew like this. It's dangerous to be
a pretty slave. That's mostly true for the women, but
sometimes for boys, too. We've all known someone
who takes a knife to her own face so that she can
save herself. Afterward, we tell her the scars are more
beautiful than the smooth skin that was there before. I
think the grown-ups really mean it, but the Egyptians
don't agree, which is what Amma calls a blessing.

I'm so caught up in looking at her that I barely hear
what they're all talking about.

"Bring it over," the woman in the water says as she
walks closer to the other girls.

Unlike before, they don't try to stay dry when they
approach her. They don't even take off their clothes or
jewelry before stepping into the water.

"Open it," she says when they're finally in front of
her. It's the smallest girl who reaches over and pulls the
top off the basket. All three girls step back from it, as
if it had a poisonous snake inside, but the one they call
Mistress reaches in and picks the baby up. She holds
him out in front of her and looks at him for a long
time. Even her stare must have something special in it,
because he stops crying and looks back at her, as if he's
curious to see who this person is. Babies can't really do

that, but that's what it looks like.

"We'll take him home with us," she says at last, and then lays him back down in the basket.

The girls look scared. "But Mistress," the one with the pink face says, and then stops as if something was shoved into her mouth.

The tall one just stands there looking at everything but her mistress. It's the small one who finally says, "Surely, Mistress, this must be a—" and then she stops.

"A what?" her mistress says. My Amma has done that to me, almost like she's daring and expecting me to answer at the same time. These girls can't just say "nothing" or "forget it" to her, like I do sometimes when Amma's voice gets all gravelly like that and I know I'm about to get punished for something.

The small girl looks down and then up at her mistress. She must think she has to be very brave to do it, because she blurts, "Surely this is a Hebrew child."

Her mistress just looks at her, waiting to hear more.

The tall girl steps in. I think she must be a good friend, even if she is an Egyptian, because it looks like she's trying to help the other girl. "Won't your father, the blessed Pharaoh, be very angry if you bring this boy home?"

I jump back. It's lucky I'm in the reeds where they can't see or hear me. The daughter of the Pharaoh, I tell myself. The Egyptians say he's the son of a god. Amma

always spits when someone mentions that and says,
"Nonsense." None of the Hebrews believe it, but here's
this golden lady standing right in front of me, every bit
of her body uncovered for me to see, and I wonder if
there's more to the story than I know. It seems to me
that only a god could make someone like this.

I don't realize it, but I've stood up. I'll be ashamed
to tell Amma this later, because it's not on account of
the baby. I don't know how I'll tell her that I just about
forgot the baby. It's as if that woman, the Pharaoh's
daughter, has told me to rise without even looking at
me. I'm pretty sure she doesn't know I'm there, and yet
it's like she commanded my body anyway.

They're all walking through the water to the bank
now. One of the girls is carrying the basket with my
baby brother in it. All three girls struggle to get out
of the water. They had to walk in a lot further to get
to where their mistress was standing than they did to
pick up the basket. They're weighed down by their wet
clothes and jewelry, but the Pharaoh's daughter keeps
rising, all of her shimmering and gold against the green
trees and reeds. The tallest girl rushes as fast as she
can to bring a cloth to her mistress and wipes down
her arms, legs, back, and stomach. She bends down
and lifts each her mistress's feet and rubs it gently, then
puts the whitest looking dress over her head. I thought
the other girls were clean, but this makes me almost

want to cry it's so perfectly white, like the clouds that sometimes look like they're dancing across the sky.

One of the other girls brings a golden stool and she sits. Then the tall girl begins to comb her hair out, bit by bit. I've always wanted a comb. I imagine how good that would feel, and how nice my hair would be. Amma tries to run her fingers through my hair to untangle it after I spend all day running. The wind pushes it around, and dust gets all the way into it, but no matter what she does it's always a wild tangle, like a dust cloud that I carry around with me all the time.

This comb is white and pink and blue all at once. Amma and Baba always tell me, "Slaves don't have the luxury to believe in miracles," but they've never seen anything like this comb. I can't believe something can shimmer and change color but stay the same all at once.

The Pharaoh's daughter must have thought about what her girls said, because she says, "He is not a Hebrew," and I can't tell if she really believes that or just won't hear anyone tell her she's wrong. "He has no mother and no father. He was born of the water. You saw it yourselves."

The girls are pretty confused about that, but they all nod. It's stupid. I know he's a Hebrew. I saw my Amma's belly get big and heavy with my own eyes and then watched her bring him into life. She's his mother, not this river.

"All things born of the river are sacred," she says, and again the girls look like they don't understand what she's saying. I don't either. I've heard a lot of crazy Egyptian things, but I never heard anything like this before. I look closely at her, and then I wonder if she's making that up, even though her face looks exactly like it did before.

Well, not exactly. As they're talking, the girls pile gold on her. She's wrapped in it, over her dress and around her waist, her neck, her ankles and wrists, and on every one of her fingers. They paint her eyes black like theirs, and put red onto her lips so that they look like blood. Instead of one of those bands that each of them are wearing, they put a headdress on her. I watch them do it, and it's just about the most complicated thing I've ever seen. First, they take parts of her hair and pin it to the top of her head, crossing the pieces so that it looks like the basket my brother is in, then they weave golden cloth through it and tie that to the headdress, which they lower onto her whole head. It's covered in jewels that ring around her head like a crown. I think that the gem in the middle of her forehead must be the biggest, greenest one in the entire world.

All the while, she keeps talking, "We will take him home. He will be our son, and a member of the royal house. My father respects all divinity. He will understand the miracle of this boy's birth."

When they're done with her she looks like a goddess for real. I see that my hand has reached out, as if to touch her, to feel all that shining gold and know what it means to hold something precious.

I'm still standing in the reeds. I must look like I grew out of them. There's dirt on my face. My hair is tangled as always. There are tears in my dress that Amma has sewn back up a hundred times. All that usually makes me invisible. I think there must be something wrong with Egyptians' eyes, because they usually can't see me until one of them needs to send me on an errand. But the Pharaoh's daughter must see more than they do, because she looks over at me as if she knew I was there all along. Her blood-red mouth stretches out into a smile. She moves her hand so little that only I see it. I'm not sure how she tells me, but I know she's calling me over to her, just like she called the other girls. I know that she will save us all.

The sun she carries around with her shines brighter than ever. It sparkles hot and perfect. It's mine to lay my hand on. I take my first step toward her.

# THE WATERY SEASON

*"So Sarai, Abram's wife, took her maid,*
*Hagar the Egyptian—after Abram had dwelt in*
*the land of Canaan ten years—*
*and gave her to her husband as concubine.*
*He cohabited with Hagar and she conceived; and*
*when she saw that she had conceived,*
*her mistress was lowered in her esteem."*
Genesis 16:3-4

———◆———

The signs were all right there in front of her. The wind blew the oak leaves above her head. The white flowers that dotted the hillside had pushed their small heads up. The sun rose higher and higher, reminded her of the purple lilies rising above the water when the god awoke, sinking back down when it was time to sleep. She hadn't seen those flowers in ten years, and though she didn't remember the way back, she knew she had been brought north and west to get here. She just had to reverse course, head southeast to reach her home.

There were many things Hagar didn't understand. How the water stayed in the well even after a stone had gone through it. What happened to the fire after it had burnt to embers. Why one bird always veered away from the group when the rest flocked across the sky. Her mother told her they could find signs in everything, that each motion of the earth and sun had something to teach, but where she saw portents of a bad batch of bread or a good year, Hagar saw patterns that added up to the world's random wonder.

What she understood least of all was how she had ended up here, so far from a river after a childhood on the flood plain of the Nile. For eleven years she had stayed close to her mother's skirts, had done as she was told to the best of her ability. Which often wasn't good enough.

People called her stupid. Her brothers, the women in the market who tried to confuse her into bringing home more flour than her mother asked for, even her mother, who said her daughter's eyes were not empty but filled with dreams, whispered it into her hair, and loved her anyway. Her mother, who put her arm around Hagar's shoulders whenever the local children laughed at her, who pushed Hagar behind her big, round bottom when her father came at her, ready with his closed fist, and wouldn't let him approach.

Her mother wasn't always quick enough. Sometimes, Hagar saw the weariness pass across her mother's face when her father started raging. At those moments she thought her mother must be too tired to even raise her arms or offer protection. If she concentrated hard she could still feel his slap across her ear, the one that came after she spilled the mash and ruined the beer, or couldn't figure out how to stitch the rips in the men's clothes back up, or when she forgot her tasks and stared out into the water, waiting to see if she could spot the start of its yearly rise.

Hagar loved the watery season, when the fields flooded and the date palms sagged with fruit. The mud was so thick then that her father was happy. "People always need bricks," he would say, and head out with her brothers to see who would hire them. The birds liked high water too. They came in flocks so thick the sky sometimes turned white with their wings. If he got lucky, her father would trap one to sell at the temple. Hagar had never tasted bird flesh, but rich people prized it, would pay enough for a live goose to tide the family over during the dry months.

But the rains didn't always come, and the river didn't always rise enough. Then, her mother told her Lord Hapi was angry, and the frogs stopped their singing, the flies sat stunned on the dry banks. When the rains didn't come, and the river didn't rise, the papyrus dried out, and her father went out each day to work, and came home at midday with an empty purse. During those times, her parents fought. She could hear their voices, loud and full of anger, from where she sat outside. Her father would accuse his wife of treachery, of having a diseased womb that gave him a baby who looked normal. He had already planned her wedding and the dowry it would bring in, but then she turned out to be an imbecile and useless. "If I had known," he said, "I would have left her out for the crocodiles." He would rail against the rich men whose whims determined the course of his life, how stingy they became when things didn't go as they'd hoped. "The wrong men get all the fortune," he'd say. "They bribe the gods, but it's all wasted on them. Look at me! Strong and healthy, but stuck here with only one deceptive wife and a drooling girl-child hanging on her apron."

Hagar didn't understand why he would say that. She lifted her hand to her mouth, but she knew even before doing so that he was wrong. There was no drool on her chin. Her mother had taught her to keep it inside her mouth, to swallow it down. She remembered her mother saying, "Men like your father cannot see the world before them. He lives in dreams, like you, only his blind him to the world as it is."

Her father was still ranting, "I deserved better than this. I deserved the palaces. It should have been me surrounded by beautiful wives and dozens of children making my name for me."

"You?" her mother would scoff, "who digs in the mud and makes bricks? Who cuts the papyrus, only to hand it off to others with the skill to make use of it?" Her own father had been a merchant once. She had hoped to marry a scholar, but a daughter's fate depends on her father's continued success, which is how she ended up here, in a mud hut filled with dust and stale sweat. "The gods have already given you everything and more than you deserve."

At times like that, when her parents spat in each other's faces, and her mother told her to look for signs of prosperity in the feathers that fell from the birds as they passed overhead, or the patterns of mud and dried-out silt at the edge of the reeds, her brothers would cuff Hagar's face anytime they happened to pass by, and then they, too, would laugh at her, even though they'd always chase off the other boys who tried to look up her dress or confuse her with their tricks.

During the dry years, Hagar had to stay very quiet. She had to keep out of everyone's way. But the year she turned twelve, her body stopped wanting to be hidden. Her skirts got shorter, her tunics tighter, and no one noticed for all the fighting, until the day the boy next door, who had suckled with her, their mothers sitting side by side in the afternoon sun, promised her a jewel he'd pulled from the bottom of the mud if she came with him into the high reeds, until he'd tried to put his hand under her dress and made a funny face. That's where her brothers found them, and she smiled at them, as she always did, wondering at the new game the neighbor boy would play.

She cried all the way home, telling them she wanted her jewel, but they dragged her home to their mother, then turned back around and left. When they came back, their knuckles were bruised, and she saw she'd have to mend their clothes again. She hoped she'd sew them well.

Her mother began crying over her, asking, "What will happen to you, my stupid, dreamy girl?" Each night, she would hear whispers from her parents' bed at night. Hagar couldn't hear what they were saying, but she knew they were talking about her. They were always talking about her.

After that, her mother would try to teach her something new each day, each week. How to build a fire, which made Hagar swell like a frog with pride, because no one had ever let her come near a flame before.

How to cook a full meal. Her father shouted that it was taking too long, that she was too slow to learn anything, that she made too many mistakes. Her brothers threw the food she cooked on the floor in disgust, but her mother stroked her hair, said, "Don't worry, you're getting better every day. It takes everyone time to learn," and then tears would leak out of her eyes, which she'd hide from Hagar's father. Hagar would watch her wipe them quickly and say, all business again, "Let's try that again."

Then she was here. With these old people who needed help with everything. She had her own knife now, and hardly ever nicked herself anymore. She cooked for them, and slept on the floor next to her mistress, who had bad dreams and needed water brought to her in the middle of the night. In the morning, Hagar would help unfold the old lady into the day, rubbing each creaking joint until it could swing on its own. "You are as slow as the heat of the day," her mistress would say, "but your touch is full of magic." Then she'd rise and walk back and forth in the tent, ankles cracking, knees seizing, hips bent over, until she could stand and walk, though she had nowhere to go.

Hagar didn't understand how there could be so much life in a place with no river, or how they could all eat so well without the thick papyrus to cook and fish to catch. The trees that grew dark green and broad shaded their tents. From there, she could see where the locals had cut away the trees to make room for the neat rows of grain that grew on small farms, and the sheep grazing in empty pastures. Even without flowing water, the beetles had shiny backs. She would watch them crawl across the hard ground, looking for small seams in the crumbly dirt. There were no crocodiles here, but her mistress told her to beware the snakes and scorpions, so she watched for them, stayed back when they raised their fearsome heads, or else tried to hit them with the sharp edge of her knife to see if she could cut them cleanly in two.

She wondered if her mother thought of her. Or her father, who looked at her hips and thighs, said he could finally find a use for her, and handed her over to the traders. By the time they gave up on the river that year, her father accused her mother of stretching things out, of trying to cheat him out of a decent profit. He declared Hagar ready. Hagar didn't know what he meant, but she followed her parents out of the house, where she saw a group of men, their heads draped in long cloths, each like a minor pharaoh. She watched one of the men, a long knife tucked into the rope tied around his waist, put a bag of coins into her father's hand. Her mother stood very still while the men talked, then turned to Hagar, took her now plump shoulders in her hands, told her to be a good girl, and then turned and called her brothers in for dinner.

One of the men took Hagar by the arm, told her to get into a cart that was hitched to an ugly ass and stay quiet. At first, she was happy to feel the bump of the wheels underneath her. She looked around with wonder at these places beyond walking distance from her small house and so beyond the far reaches of her imagination. She wondered how long this trip would be, grew sad when the hours stretched into sunset, then afraid when they didn't head back for home. She cried for her mother, thinking the men would understand and turn around, but they just shouted at her to keep her voice down. That her noise was bad for business.

The caravan traveled for days, picking up other women. They were tied together at the waist by a thick rope, walked in a shuffling line most of the day, but the traders let them sleep in the cart at night. Hagar was smaller and younger than the others. None of the other women seemed to notice her, but they made sure she was never pulled into the cart by one or more of the traders at dusk. Each time, Hagar listened as the wheels squeaked, the cart rocked back and forth, and then followed the others into it when the men called for them, felt their hands squeeze her skin, rub up next to her, and then let her be.

Hagar was lonely on the road. Only the traders spoke her language, and they didn't talk to the women, except to order them in and out of the cart. The other

women didn't try to talk to her. Each kept to herself,
absorbed in her own history of misery as if to guard
against the pain of another separation that would come
when they were sold off the caravan one by one.

Hagar still cried for home at night, but she was
afraid of the man with the long knife and hid her sobs.
She remembered that her mother had told her to be
good, and so she choked back her tears, thought if she
was good enough, she would be sent home again. She
repeated it over and over to herself, "Be a good girl, and
you'll go home," until, after two days, she went from
hoping it would be true to believing it would happen.
She believed in it the way her father had believed in
his gods, had stepped out of the road when a cow, eyes
shining like the goddess's, sacred udders swinging
beneath its belly, was led through the town by its owner.

By the time they reached this new land, Hagar
had lost count of how long they'd been walking. They
stayed close to the sluggish Nile, then went through
vast, desert caverns, stopped whenever they passed a
town or well, and finally reached a city that seemed to
fill the entire valley, its ends reaching from mountain to
mountain in every direction.

Hagar had never seen so many people in one place
before. She had run back and forth to the local market
for her mother many times. When the traders told the
girls they'd arrive at the market soon, Hagar thought

she would recognize it, but this was nothing like the collection of threadbare men and women, each with a single basket, selling and buying what they could to survive. Here, a person could buy and sell everything. Textiles, cattle, people. She wanted to wander around, touch the colorful spices, look at the strange faces. Some of the men had long braids winding down their backs. She saw others with black markings across their cheeks and, most wondrous of all, boys and girls with eyes the color of the sky. But the traders kept the women tied together in the cart from the moment they entered the town, so Hagar had to settle for watching as the swirl of activity passed around her.

The traders had sold most of the other women by the time a couple came out to inspect their wares. Hagar's first impression of the woman who would become her mistress was that she seemed impossibly old. The hair at her forehead where it stuck out from beneath her hood looked like wispy clouds above skin veined with blue. But Hagar had been taught that people who lived to be that old must be wise and protected by the gods, so she didn't cry out when the woman pinched her cheeks or pulled down her lips to inspect her teeth or her dress to examine her body.

"That one's father said she's a simpleton," one of the traders said. "But we haven't had any trouble with her." When both the man and woman spoke to her in

Egyptian, Hagar was happy to be picked. They spoke their own language with each other, though, and Hagar never could form her mouth around the strange round sounds they used. So she waited until they spoke to her, and got used to listening to their gibberish. Sometimes, she could pretend they were the frogs of her home, talking to her like they used to.

There was much to see here, more things than she thought possible in the world. Without a river, the slave girls had to walk back and forth to the well, and everyone prayed for rain during the fall, then shivered as it fell in winter. No monkeys chattered in the trees, but hawks flew and swooped overhead, and crows called back and forth to one another from the tops of the cypress trees.

Hagar still tried to be good, even though she spilled the food and dropped the firewood sometimes, but her mistress was patient, more patient than Hagar's parents had been. No one told her to stay away from the fire here, and in time she became strong enough to balance the heavy water jug on her head like the other girls did.

Soon, her mistress told her she'd be sleeping in her master's tent. Hagar asked if she would be kneading his joints into motion every morning, too, but her mistress only laughed. "Oh, you are a child," she said. "Just do as he says." So she entered his tent, and every night he lay his old body on top of hers. She could feel the bones of his pelvis, see his ribs and collarbone through the thin skin that lay over them. She still didn't really understand. But every night, he would climb on top again. And every night, she would wonder at how so old a man could still retain so much strength, to hold her down, to catch his breath and let it go.

She had been called stupid since the moment she could understand words, but some things she knew. When her belly grew and she became tired and her head hurt, she knew. She rejoiced at how good her body was. She turned from the old man, looked into her mistress's face, and asked, "Is this what you wanted?" Her mistress smiled, told her that she had done just right, then propped Hagar between her old legs, the skin sagging in folds around her knees and pressed against the sides of her belly to help push the boy out, cradled him to her old breast before Hagar could even hold him tight.

"Give me my son," she said, because though she didn't know much, she had seen babies search for their mothers' bodies before they even opened their eyes. "He's hungry," she said, when he began to wail, "and you can't feed him."

Her mistress didn't like that. Hagar saw her stiffen, clutch the baby tighter in her thin fingers before handing him over. "Put him up," she said, "but remember whose child this is. You are the vessel. You have your job to do. But you are no one's wife and no one's mother." Hagar wished for her own mother then, for the skirts to hide behind and her mother's sharp breath on her hair.

So this is how it would be. They would love her boy, these old people. They would love her hands on their joints and her young body doing what theirs no longer could. But they would never love her. She was just a bewildered young woman far from home. Even the old man, who had come to her night after night, had taken her like a sign of his own forgotten youth, sent her back to her mistress's tent, where she lay on the floor with their boy, ready to feed and quiet his cries. He called her mistress, "Mama," then came and demanded Hagar's breast.

He was a happy child, moving back and forth between the two women who adored him. He would tease Hagar the way the neighbor children used to at home, but she didn't mind it from him. Because she knew he needed her. Even if he got confused about what the word "mother" meant.

Her mistress was getting older. The boy's infancy and toddler years tired her out, aged her. She lost her patience more easily, criticized everything and blamed Hagar for her own increasingly aching body. As if Hagar's hands had changed when she gave birth, as if she could no longer press and rub, although Hagar didn't think they had. She looked at them when her mistress was yelling at her, but they didn't look any different.

So she tried harder, because Hagar still kept her secret faith. She still believed that if she was very good, if she did as she was told, if her master and mistress liked her, she would be sent back home. No one told her, but the more she saw, the more she knew it to be true. Other girls had disappeared from the families they served. One day they'd be gathering firewood or carrying water back from the well beside her, and the next they'd be gone and never spoken of again. She knew of nowhere else they could go other than back to their homes.

She still wished for it, her riverside home, even though she had forgotten what her brothers' faces looked like. She could no longer name the smell that attached to her mother's hands and hair. She had grown used to living in this rocky land. Now there was the boy to think about. He was growing taller and stronger. He pulled her hair sometimes and laughed in her face when she spoke to him. But she loved him and forgave him every time, continued to make his favorite dishes, to make sure his fire was lit during the cold winter nights. She wanted to go home, but she didn't want to leave him. Here was another thing Hagar didn't understand, how she could have two wishes at the same time.

Not like her mistress, who doted on her boy, treated him like a prince, heir to his father's home. Hagar felt proud of being part of that. All these flocks and land, these beautiful leather tents, would go to the son she had given them. Sometimes, Hagar caught her mistress looking at their boy. Was it sadness she saw there? Or regret? Whatever it was would disappear before she had time to study it, so she never knew. She continued to try to do a good job, to figure out how to go home and stay here, to return to her mother and to be with her boy.

Until the day she knew she had to leave. Things had changed. Her master had begun inviting her mistress into his tent. In all the years she had been there, she had never seen that before. They lay their old bodies together the way he used to do with Hagar. After, Hagar would hear her mistress sighing, telling her master he was a fool to believe that nature could be denied, and then she would return again the next night.

Her master was different from any man Hagar had ever known. He wasn't like her own father, who had stormed around their little house, with his demands and his tempers. Her master didn't stick out his chest like her father had, or sit with the other men down by the river talking loudly of his youth. Maybe her master was too old for that, Hagar thought. Or maybe he just liked sitting in his tent, waiting for the local men to come to him to try to make trades, and he opened his hands wide, as if to encompass the whole world, and thanked his God for his good fortune whenever anyone asked how he came to have so much wealth.

But Hagar watched him with those men. She saw how he waited to hear what they wanted and how much they were willing to give. She saw him weigh out their offers and give back only enough to satisfy both. It was nice that he credited his God. The traders who brought her here had told her it would be a good home because of her master's faith, that no one would hit her anymore. And she supposed this God must be very nice to help her master out as he did. But she remembered her parents' gods. They brought the rain and the floods to the Nile and made everyone happy. Those were nice gods, too, she thought.

Things were different once her mistress began to get fat. Her stomach blew up like the bladder Hagar filled with water to amuse their boy. How her mistress laughed and laughed, even though she could hardly stand up and her legs swelled up. She called for Hagar to rub her joints more than ever, and stopped complaining that she was doing it wrong. Hagar was happy, too, because her mistress was pleased with her again.

When her master explained that his God had worked a miracle, Hagar wondered anew at the strange ways of this land. She had never known gods who could change the ways of nature. Her mother had taught her to revere the gods because they made the sun rise and fall every day, made the river flood its banks in the proper season. At home, gods made sure nature's design remained unbroken. Here, her master's God broke all the rules for his benefit. For the first time, Hagar was afraid of her master, how powerful he must be, but she was happy that her boy would have a playmate, wouldn't be left alone with just the old people and her anymore.

But he didn't have a playmate. Her mistress got angry with her again after the new baby was born. Hagar wasn't allowed near the baby. Her mistress shouted for food and water and then told her to get out of the tent. She stopped paying attention to their boy, too. He didn't seem to care, because her mistress had always kept him from doing what he wanted, which was to run as fast as he could into the wadis and then jump from rock to rock until he reached the bottom. Her mistress was afraid he would hurt himself, called him down from the trees he climbed, kept him from chasing after the sheep when they ran away. Now that she was so taken with her baby, he could roam as far as he wanted.

It bothered Hagar. Her mistress didn't talk to their boy, or fawn over him as she used to. More than that, Hagar saw her mistress eye him as if he were a stranger, a trespasser on her rightful property. She didn't seem to like Hagar anymore, either. Hagar still tried to be good. She kept her knife sharp so it was ready whenever she was needed. She ran to the well and back as fast as she could with the day's water. But nothing satisfied her mistress. Hagar even heard her complain to her master, saying that they would have to get a new slave, that this one had outlasted her usefulness. Her master hadn't said anything then, just touched her mistress's hand and asked to see their baby.

There was a lot Hagar didn't understand. But when her mistress lifted her skinny arm and struck their boy across the face, she decided she had learned enough to know they wouldn't be missed if she picked up and left.

She couldn't see that he had done anything wrong. All boys are curious about their baby brothers. And children don't know their own strength. She knew that all he wanted to do was hug the baby. He just squeezed too hard. But her mistress got angry, and when he laughed at her and wouldn't give the baby back, she called him terrible names, slapped him, and then turned her anger on Hagar.

"This is all your fault, you stupid cow. I should have known better than to think anyone normal would come out of a half-wit."

Hagar hurried their boy out of her mistress's tent. Her mistress was old, and now she had a baby to look after, although there was a young woman who came and nursed him every day and slept next to him all night, so that her mistress could sleep as long as she liked.

Hagar thought back to the old people she had known at home, how they seemed to curse life with every breath, angry at still being alive or at their own diminished strength. Maybe that's what her mistress was feeling. Then Hagar felt some pity for her. Not enough to forgive her mistress for taking it out on her boy. Her boy. Hagar's boy, she thought. Not theirs. Now that her mistress had her own son, this one could be all hers. And so she decided to leave. She would take some bread, water, and the knife they had given her. She had lived with them for ten years. It was hers now, she figured, the only gift anyone had ever put into her hand.

The next morning, Hagar woke while it was still dark. She had to get to the well and back before the other slave girls arrived to see her with a small jug instead of the huge one she normally dipped down into the well then balanced on her head for the walk back to her master's tents.

The path was damp under her sandals. Usually dust spiraled around her ankles, even if she left the tent just after sunup. By then, whatever moisture the earth had made for itself overnight was already seeping back in. Hagar thought those beads of water were smart to hide during the day and only come out at night when it got cooler and the sun wouldn't bully them as it did her. She pulled her cloak around her shoulders against the cold and walked quickly, afraid of the beasts that might be out roaming. Her mistress had always told her to stay in when it was dark, that the mountain lions would want to take a bite out of her, that she'd be tasty to them. And it was too dark to see if scorpions, their fat black tails curled up, were out scurrying around, ready to strike her innocent heel.

Hagar was afraid, but she pushed her fear away, setting her jug down to make a shoving motion with her hands out in front of her, just as her mother had shown her to do when she was a child and was scared of going down to the river by herself to wash their clothes, or of her father's return at the end of the long workday, his face covered in rock chalk, his temper flaring.

After a few pushes, she felt calm again. She picked up her jug and began the long walk to the well. She hoped to have it to herself and make it back before first light, so she could hide away the water and pretend that today would be like every other day she had spent for the last ten years. She would bring food to her mistress, cut firewood, and lug water. Her mistress would probably shout at her for making a mistake with the stew, because try as she might, Hagar never did get the hang of cooking here, where they ate strange foods and let their meat sit in the pot for so long.

Hagar knew there were things she should think about before the trip, things to plan for or worry about, but she couldn't think of what they might be.

That night, she fell into a deep, exhausted sleep. Still, she rose early again the next morning. No one was

around. Not even the sun had lifted its big red eye to
stare at her. She moved quietly through the tents to
where her son lay sleeping, his mouth open, skin spongy
and slack. She picked him up out of his bed, tied him
to her back, and began to walk southwest toward the
desert. South toward home.

At first, she felt strong. She knew she was saving
her boy from a life of misery. Mothers don't like to share
their sons unless, like her, they have to. Her mistress
would turn even her master against her boy. Hagar was
sure of it. Though the new baby was soft and round and
smiled at everyone who lifted him high into the air, he
would grow into his mother's love and turn on his older
brother, too. It's what brothers do. Didn't she see her
brothers fight? When they were all young, her brothers
had invented games together and played in the reeds
and river. But as they got older, they began to eye each
other with distrust, to take a tally of who had what—
girls' attention, number of coins collected from working
the shores of the river, their father's esteem.

Hagar could see the future in her master's tents
as clearly as if it were happening that day. The slow
campaign against her boy, the way her mistress was
already turning the things they had loved about him—
his playful tricks and high energy—into signs of mischief
and wickedness. Hagar would have to sit by and watch
as he lost even his father's love. A slave girl could say

nothing against her mistress, who was, everyone said, wise with age, and had her husband's ear.

For the first time in her life, Hagar didn't want to be good. She felt angry, which kept her feet steady and her back strong for many hours. Eventually, she burned with the heat of the day and realized that she would have to find a shady spot to wait out the worst of the day and then continue her trek until nightfall.

By then, her boy had woken, demanded to be untied and allowed to stand on the ground. He called for his mama, his other mama, and Hagar had to explain that she was the only one he had left. Then he screamed at her, the same insults her mistress had hurled, "You're too stupid. You don't know anything. I want to go home."

Hagar had a lifetime of being shouted at. She was not going to be shouted at any longer. "Shut your mouth, boy," she said, shocked that such strong words could travel out of her own mouth. "I am the woman who birthed you. It was my body that fed you for the first years of your life. I kept you alive. Not her. Not that shriveled-up old woman. She's not your mama. I am."

He was taken aback too, that the mild-mannered slave who had always smilingly been the butt of his practical jokes and cruel barbs was talking to him like this, but he was still a child, and the blows he tried to strike her with were easy enough to deflect. She let him flail until she had had enough, then pinned his arms together with her work-hardened hands, squeezed just hard enough for him to yelp that she was hurting him, and warned him, "No more hitting now. We have a long way to go." She fed him some bread and water, then curled up with him under a spike-leafed tree, inhaling the piney smell and letting her tired muscles wilt in the afternoon heat. The fight seemed to go out of the boy, too.

He whimpered by her side for a time, then whispered, "Why doesn't she want me anymore?"

"She loves her new baby more," Hagar answered. "You were born of a slave, and he was born of a rich and free woman. I wasn't always a slave, though. I had a family, too. Now, we're going home to them. To our real home, where you can play in the marsh by the river like the other boys." She saw that he was trying to be a little man, hold back his tears, but she had never understood what good that would do. "Cry now, boy. It's okay. I cried when they took me from my home, too. But you'll see. It will be better where we're going."

So he did, and then they waited, dozing and waking, their skin slicked with sweat that evaporated in the dry air the moment they stood up from under the tree's shade to stretch their limbs. She fed him more bread and water, drank some herself, and when she felt a slight shift in the air, took his hand and continued heading south.

She thought they would have to walk until it got too dark to see and then find a place to sleep. Hagar looked around. They would need firewood. She was thankful to have her knife then, used it to cut sticks from thick bushes along their path that she bundled and draped over her boy's small back.

"It's heavy," he complained. "I don't want to carry these."

"It won't be for long," she said, thinking that they had spoiled him, his two doting mothers, that this trip would be good for him, teach him the lessons her own mother had passed along—that we live in a great web of stars and earth and sea. That there is a line through everything, holding it all together. We can't see it, but the gods know it's there. It tethers them to the ground. That's why they like the sacrifices that people bring, because they get hungry and can't range out to find meat on their own. But her mother showed her that everything in life was like that. Carrying water from the well to the house, which was dry, brought water and land together. Rain was the heaven's way of reuniting with the earth.

And now, carrying those sticks, the boy became part of it. They would burn the wood to ash and watch the smoke rise, the earth connecting with sky.

Hagar told the boy all this as they walked. He had

never heard any of it, because his father, her old master, worshipped a God who didn't like the gods of her youth. Hagar had heard her master teaching her boy about his own God, how He had spoken to her master, intervened on his behalf with men and nature, and so they must worship Him and love him.

But she was going home now, where her master's God didn't live, and her mother's did. So the boy had to know. He was so young, but already he understood more than she did. He would have to learn so many things when they got home. The least she could do was tell him the stories she remembered.

He wouldn't listen. Every time she stopped talking he said, "They'll come to look for us. They'll catch us and take you back and beat you for being so bad. My real parents won't let you get away with this."

"Oh, my love," Hagar said, wondering how long it would take for him to forget that other mother, the one who had already replaced him with a better son, "They won't come. The gods will hear me. They will keep us on our narrow road."

They slept that night, huddled together against the cold, his head cradled in her arms for the first time since he weaned. Hagar felt chilled through. She worried that she wouldn't find her way. She was scared of what kinds of people they might meet along the way, but she felt that some god—either her master's or her own—must be protecting them, because the boy's warm breath against her collarbone, his hand curled under her arm, were the softest things she had ever felt. It's true he had cried again, "I want my mama. Not you. You're not my mother. I want my real mother. And my father." He picked up small rocks that lay on the ground and threw them at her, stomped his feet, his face turned red and angry, his voice louder and full of the pain only a small boy can summon.

"I want to go home," he said again, but Hagar didn't understand. "We are going home," she said, trying to make him see, and she thought of the papyrus growing six feet tall by the edge of the river, the deep black mud of its banks in winter.

He'd cried for a while after that, but for all his complaints, she was known to him, familiar as his own skin, and when she pulled him into her lap, some memory of infancy must have flooded his body, because he allowed his limbs to relax, his breathing to slow, and he slept, cradled by the mother he had long ago rejected.

They rose early the next morning, the boy still half asleep when Hagar set him on his feet and led him by the hand down into the valley ahead of them. That first day, they stopped at every well they passed. Hagar refilled the jug, and they both drank deeply. In the morning, a woman took pity on them and let them rest in her barn. At night, they found a cave to sleep in.

The next day, they walked until the land began to slope down. By midday, they had left the craggy mountains, crossed into the desert of the Negev, where the sun, unmerciful before, became a source of torture. Few people traveled here. Even caravans were scarce. And, Hagar noted, their water was running low. She would have to find a well, but there was no sign of one nearby, no hint of green along the ground that would betray an underground spring.

So they kept walking. During the worst of the heat, they hid under the sparse shade of an acacia bush. By evening the water was gone. But they had another night's fire to warm them from the ice the desert sent through them once the sun went down—and they woke to walk again well before the sun had time to stretch and rise.

It was harder that day. Hagar still carried the jug, hoping to see a well to replenish their store and feed her boy, who had cried himself to sleep again the night before but seemed to wither as the day wore on, too worn out to complain or berate her, too weak to carry the sticks she cut whenever they passed a bush with limbs that would burn well. She began to see things. Cows lying dead by the side of the road that turned out to be bits of twig and dust. Twice she thought she saw a well and ran to it, only to find that it was nothing, just a shimmery spot on the horizon, a trick of the light or the gods. But they wouldn't toy with her like that, she thought. Not when she was trying to get home, to take her boy away from the pain he was sure to know in the future.

They kept walking, the earth beneath them cracked and dry. The only other beings they saw were scavenger birds circling above and a snake sunning itself. Even the snake would burrow underground when it got too hot, she knew. It would find a patch of cool under the ground to wait out the heat. And the birds would roost somewhere or find an animal the desert had killed and feast.

Eventually, the boy couldn't walk anymore, so Hagar tied him to her back again, felt how he labored to breathe, his skin as hot as the ground, and how he mumbled, cried out for his father, though Hagar could tell he wasn't aware of his own words.

Finally, she had to put him down. She felt too weak, too thirsty to keep going, and too angry that the gods would put the notion of running away into her head only to kill them here in the empty expanse of desert. The boy was almost dead. She could see that well enough, though she couldn't bear to watch the breath actually leave him.

She found the fullest bush she could and lay him beneath it. His eyes looked sunken, and when he turned his face to hers, she felt as if he was already looking past her into the afterlife. He was her prince, but there were no water lilies here to adorn his body. No water to wash away the grime of human life. She had nothing other than an empty jug to send with him on his journey. She set it down next to him, and hoped he'd find water when he got to where he was going. She turned her back, sat down just close enough to chase away the buzzards when they started to swoop in to investigate the scene.

Surely, Hagar thought, some god will hear me. Surely, if I cry loudly enough, my master's God or my mother's will listen to my plea. Her mouth parched, voice barely a croak, she called out. "I'm sorry. I'm sorry," and saw another shimmer on the horizon. There was a man standing beside it. Or above it. Her master, or her master's God. Hagar couldn't tell which. She wondered how he got here so quickly, when she had to walk for three days, always thinking their destination was around the next bend, but still there was no sign of her river home.

The man didn't speak, but she felt him beckon to her. Afraid she would be punished, Hagar sat still, staring at the shimmer, then the man, then the shimmer again. Then she knew he was like the dead cows, a sign that would disappear the closer she got. She hadn't understood those, and she didn't understand this one. She was scared and alone, and the expanse of sandy rock all around hurt her eyes.

"You won't trick me again," she shouted as loudly as she could manage. "I know your ways now. But I am a poor woman with nothing left to give you. So take my boy and love him better than I could." Except the spot in the distance kept shimmering, and though she thought it would be another patch of dry ground, Hagar felt pulled by thirst and the man who beckoned to her. She dragged her tired body on hands and knees. She had to be sure this was a deception, the last one, she knew, that would ever be played upon her.

On any other day, she would have noticed that her palms and knees, though they started on hard rock, were soon cushioned by a thin layer of moss, that the ground was springing back up under her weight, if only a little. That day, though, she felt her attention split in two—the mirage ahead of her, the boy behind—so that she felt the moisture touch her fingertips before she registered what it was.

"Water," she said, amazed. She bent her head and lapped at it like a dog, scooped it in her hands and ran to rub it on her son's hot brow, the back of his neck. Then she grabbed the jug, ran back to the small puddle, filled it as high as it would go, and ran back to her son, who still lay dying under the bush. Hagar poured the water over his head, down his back, and ladled it into his mouth, trying not to let any drops slip through the spaces between her fingers.

Slowly, the color returned to his cheeks. He vomited once, then again, opened his eyes and looked at her, confused but no longer delirious. "Mama?" he said. When he saw who was with him, that it was Hagar, he began to cry. At first, Hagar laughed in relief to see tears form in his eyes and fall down his dusty cheeks. He would live. The gods did listen. They saved him for a reason, she thought. She looked at her boy with a new sense of wonder. There is greatness coming to him, she knew, and she had played a part in it. She chased the vultures away for good and laughed again as she felt the wind moved by their enormous wings.

She looked back over to the shallow well, thought she saw the outline of the man who had been so clear just a few moments before, and finally understood. She had no past. It had been erased by the bag of coins the trader had placed into her father's hands. All she could do was be with her boy, teach him to live with the family he had been given, the one she had been given no choice in joining, but whose fate was his, and now her own. Hagar filled her jug again, set it on her head, lifted her son, and turned north, for the long walk back home.

# ZERESH, HIS WIFE

*"There Haman told his wife Zeresh and all his
friends everything that had befallen him,
'If Mordechai, before whom you have begun to fall,
is of Jewish stock, you will not overcome him; you
will fall before him to your ruin.'"*
Esther 6:13

———— • ————

Where is that tutor? she wondered, as her sons
chased each other through their gardens,
jumping over the low walls that snaked
through the property.

"Just don't pull down the vines," she called after
them, watching as they grabbed onto anything within
reach to give themselves a boost. Let them laugh now,

she thought. They'll have to be serious soon enough. The sons of the king's chief advisor have to live up to very high expectations, even the littlest one.

"It's not fair. I can't climb over this part. Wait for me!" Poor boy, trying to keep up with his brothers, but how can seven-year-old legs move fast enough to keep up with the older ones? She could see the tears begin to well in his eyes and how quickly he tried to suppress them. He'd be another little man before long. She had given her husband a house full of sons, but she wanted this one to stay with her, a boy with smooth skin and a high, little voice.

Childish anger is the funniest kind, she thought not for the first time, but I shouldn't laugh. Poor thing. Stuck here on the wrong side of the wall with a woman and servants.

The boy was too young and angry to see what she did, how good it was to be back in Susa, her favorite court city, after a long summer. Everyone else marveled at Persepolis, but she felt relief when they left each year. The buildings and art were magnificent there, but they were built on a scale fit for gods, not men. Things were simpler in Susa. Winter here promised citrus trees, climbing ivy on the fortress walls, figs dropping seamed and sweet onto the ground.

A breeze blew through the courtyard. Her head man, old enough to have served in her grandfather's house, ordered his workers around with the rigid authority of a man half his age. His spine was still straight. His mind and eyes were clear. He was, she thought, a marvel. Proof of the Creator's goodness, although she'd never share that with anyone else. He was, after all, just a servant, and not even a Persian by birth.

It had been a long journey. The horses and mules were tired. Her sons were excited to be off the road and back in their house, with its connected gardens and buildings that wound up the hill from the road. They were also ready to settle down for the season.

When she arrived, the compound had looked uninhabited, even though her husband had come weeks in advance to prepare the palace for the king's arrival, bringing their eldest son with him. Not that it was apparent from the state of their home. Walking through, she felt as if ghosts had been floating through rather than people with the important work of the empire to do. It will take a few days to settle in, she thought. They hadn't even seen her husband yet. He was at the court, of course. He had probably been there every spare moment, no time to order the furniture to be aired or tell the maids to go out behind the kitchen wall to beat the dust out of the rugs.

Once she arrived, the work of their home got done, although it was hard with such a boisterous group of boys getting in everyone's way. Only she, or that damned tutor, if she could find him, could rein them in. The servants would never dare complain about the vizier's sons.

She shouldn't have worried. A wave of pleasure passed through her as her older boys, teenagers who would run heedless over any obstacle, stopped their game to come back and help their youngest brother over the wall. Her husband would be proud of the boys she was raising for him.

She had known, of course, that he'd be more occupied once he took his new position. It's what she had wanted and worked toward for so long. She had to remind herself of that. Now that he woke at dawn to be first at the palace should their king need him, she was left largely to herself.

How things had changed in a year. Back then she could only imagine how life would be when she had urged him to become all he could. It was a year ago to the day, or maybe the week, she realized, since they'd seen the opportunity for his advancement drop neatly into their hands.

———— ◆ ————

That morning, the sky broke blue with high strings of cloud that skittered across its surface. Preoccupied with her work and the visions she had for how high her family could climb, she hadn't noticed them.

The air smelled of dust. It was the first thing she noticed when her husband rushed into her rooms to wake her. The maid had already pulled back the curtains, and she could smell the gardens through the open window. The sky was bright, and the air smelled. Usually Susa's breezes carried the damp rich of winter, but here was summer's dust.

The previous day had been cold. She'd directed the gardeners to wrap the trees so they wouldn't shrivel and drop their fruit too early. Just a week before she had swaddled herself in thick cloaks to walk her orchards and inspect her fields. But that morning, she struggled awake in the shaft of sunlight that fell, just as she liked it, onto her bed in these early hours.

Her husband was shouting, but it was hard to tell if he was jubilant or angry. "He'll bankrupt himself this time, for sure."

His outline blurred against the bright light.

"Wake up, my dear. Big news. You'll never guess how much our lord, the king has spent on this week of feasts. He's running through the entire treasury."

That was news to bring her awake with a start.

"Are you sure?"

"Just talk for now, but court gossip is usually right about these things."

Zeresh flung away her blankets, the quilting making

a new pattern of oranges and reds as the fabric folded over itself. Gold thread snaked along its entire length. She called to her chambermaid, demanded her best clothes.

"I'll go talk to my sister. This could be just the moment we've been waiting for." Rushing past him to her dressing room, Zeresh stopped, looked back at him. Even when her father had presented this man to her as a potential suitor he had been short, his current stoutness foretold in his lean but stocky body. As usual, he was dressed in the most opulent silks and had oiled his hair to mask the thinning on top. But his beard was still thick and coiled. His vanity will be the ruin of him, she thought.

But she didn't wonder whether he could follow through on their shared goals. They had floated in the mid-level air of the court for too long, just another couple with money and lands but without the king's ear. She had watched for years as others rose in rank around them. Each time a man was appointed to the cabinet, he'd enter into a secret fraternity, the only one that mattered, one Zeresh could never enter. Instead, she watched the wives intently, noticed their false modesty when they talked about their husbands. "Now that he's minister," they'd say, "we hardly ever see him," and then they'd raise the finest wines to their satisfied lips.

Now it would be her turn. She had a good feeling

this time. She dressed carefully, perfumed her skin, the part in her hair. Her wrists clinked with piles of silver and gold bracelets. Her husband met her at the door, walked with her through the front garden, but they didn't speak. They both knew her errand. Oranges released their scent into the air.

Finally, she spoke. "Don't do anything until I get back," she ordered. "Once I find out what's real and what's just talk, we can think about how to proceed."

She rose onto her horse, was led through the quiet streets of Susa. Somewhere in the city, the market would already be busy, loud with buying and selling. Her own merchants would be there by now, getting the best prices they could on her grapes. But she rode through the early morning in the quiet precincts of wealth. On either side of her lay great estates where the women would still be doused in dreams, the men finishing their early plates of bread and olives. Only the servants stirred, doing the work that kept these places functioning.

A laborer cut back the grass with a sickle outside the wall of a large but unadorned estate. Another stood behind him, whitewashing the wall. Neither looked up as she passed.

She sniffed at the air again. The dates would be at their plumpest. She'd have to visit the orchards again after this trip to the palace.

The king's palace stood shining on the city's highest plateau, where it was visible from every precinct. She could see it ahead of her becoming larger in her sight as she rode up and around to the back entrance. Guards stopped her at the gate, but when she pulled back her veil, they quickly allowed her to ride through.

The palace grounds lay still. She never knew how they did it. Even after six nights of feasting, every noble and rich man in the province invited to drink himself into a stupor and then led to sleep it off somewhere in the side houses' many apartments, the grass was even and full. No twig hung broken from a tree. The flowers grew tall and riotous. As many times as she had passed through, she had never seen a man take a tool to hand. No gardeners bent over in toil.

Perhaps, she thought, the king really is the son of the Creator. Maybe he sends his angels to smooth over the ground at night so as not to bother the people within.

Silly thoughts, even if they helped calm her nerves. She shook them off by the time she reached the women's building and descended off her horse to the ground. Even here, where everything spread out like a field of gems, the soil lay ashy beneath her slipper, and beneath that was the winter's wet earth.

The eunuch who pulled back the heavy door smiled brightly when he saw who it was. He smiled even more when she pressed a small, gold-edged mirror into his hand. They were always happy to see her here.

He led her quietly through rooms filled with pretty young women, most of them placid-faced and bored, all the royal concubines anointed and painted for another day of waiting to see if the king would call them. He usually didn't, so they submitted themselves to the army of attendant eunuchs around them, and then had it all washed off when night came. They'd wake in the morning to do it all over again.

——— • ———

Three nights before, all the aristocratic wives and daughters had feasted together, invited by the queen to celebrate their yearly return to Susa. The king was intent on celebrating for the entire week, but the queen had tired of the festivities. The women, she knew, needed to get back to their work. Households, fields, and tenant disputes wouldn't wait on them for seven days, so she served the cakes and set them free. Let the men drink themselves stupid. Women had work to do.

Zeresh walked through these familiar rooms, pressing small gifts into the hands of the eunuchs as she passed. The wooden walls hung with heavy drapery. Jewels inlay every possible surface. It was all as if to make up for the fact that these women, plucked out of obscurity when youth still rouged their cheeks, would never have husbands of their own.

Her sister waited for her in the farthest room. As always, Zeresh was struck by her beauty. Long regal nose above thick lips. Black hair and hooded brown eyes that looked at everything as if from a distance no one could bridge. Zeresh shared every one of those features, but on her they resulted in what others called handsomeness. On her sister, they took on the solidity of fact, her radiance so obvious it had never occurred to Zeresh to feel jealous.

Her sister's looks had been good for them all. Their father had found good marriages for them both. She had married a rich man who gave her many sons. Vashti became queen.

In public, Zeresh would have scraped and bowed, put on a show about the queen's great beauty and wisdom, would have proclaimed herself unworthy to touch the great queen's hem. But this was private, two sisters who knew one another too well for that kind artifice.

She did know enough not to rush the conversation. Zeresh's characteristic forthrightness irritated her sister, and right now, she could not afford to be irritated.

"Who's the new boy?" Zeresh asked, looking over at the young man standing by the far wall. She had brought trinkets to hand out, but she hadn't known of this one's existence. By the time she saw him, her hands were empty.

"Artakama. Brought in only a few months ago. Isn't he lovely?"

He was. He was also young enough to be her oldest son, with light brown hair curling over his shoulders and large green eyes. Like all the eunuchs in the harem, he took care to tailor his looks to a woman's eye. But this one had an older man's confidence. His mouth seemed to smile even as it stayed perfectly still.

"He's my new favorite," the queen said.

"Are you feeling the need for a son these days?"

Vashti laughed off that idea. "The king is very taken with his dancing girls right now. And this one has, you'll notice, long, beautiful fingers."

Zeresh often wondered what the men in the adjoining buildings really knew of what went on in the women's building. They were brilliant men, of course, the leaders of a vast empire, but they had their preoccupations and were too confident in their own virility. The only thing a eunuch couldn't do was impregnate. Surely, she thought, the men couldn't be so caught up in their own ideas to know that castration does not strip a man of other skills.

Finally, Zeresh thought she had spent enough time thinking about her sister's pleasures to get to the point.

"Is it true?" she asked.

Vashti, attentive as always, was slow to answer. "Is

what true?"

"Is the king's feast to be the end of the treasury?"

"Quite possibly. But they all seem to lead that way, and then he manages to figure something out."

"You seem quite sanguine about it."

"What business is it of mine? He'll have enough to keep this harem standing. Enough for the next round of battles and celebrations. Enough to ransom the prettiest girls from lands far and near. Only he grows tired of them, and I am left to care for them as they grow restless and bitter when they realize that they will never leave or take my place."

It was a distraction, this complaint of her sister's. They both knew why Zeresh was there, and it wasn't to talk about palace intrigue. Zeresh had stopped caring how many virgins her king took to his bed long ago.

"This time could be different," Zeresh said.

"It could, I suppose."

"Will you speak for us, if it is?"

Interest flashed in Vashti's eyes, so brief a stranger would have missed it, but the queen had finally heard what she had been waiting for. "Dear sister," she said, the very tips of her lips lifting, "you are too focused on getting ahead. Why not be happy with your wealth, your children, your gardens? Surely, you wouldn't rather have all this."

She gave a weak wave, taking in the deep couches

and lavish fabrics that, to an untrained eye, could hide the fact that there were no windows facing out into the palace grounds. All Vashti, the most powerful woman in Persia, could see were the king's many concubines bathing in the courtyard pool. "You have your freedom, Zeresh. Freedom and industry. You do not live at the whim of an intemperate man-child whose greatest talents are killing and drinking."

"That's easy for someone with a crown on her head to say."

Vashti considered this for a moment. It looked to Zeresh as if she was thinking about a detail that had never crossed her mind before. Finally, she said, "I see that nothing I say will make you understand. Very well. You will get what you want. The eunuchs have been attending the nightly feasts. They say he has spent more on wine than would feed the city of Tyre. They sprinkle opals from the east on their meat. He has hired troops of dusky women to dance naked before them, two to every man present."

This was news to Zeresh, whose husband hadn't shared any of the details of the previous nights with her.

"Are they here, then," she asked, "swelling your ranks?"

"Now, sister, you can't think he'd bring barbarian women in here. They are taken to the brothels at daybreak. Then he brings in new girls at night. Each morning, the commoners of Susa line up to lie with women the king has touched. The Creator only knows how he will top it tonight."

Here was more news to Zeresh. But Vashti was still talking.

"So you'll have your chance. Let him sleep off his excesses for a few days, then send your man, tell him to offer the moon. He is the king. He will take it."

That was her dismissal. Vashti was finished with her. As she left, she saw her sister summoning a girl to bring wine and cheese. That new eunuch can only do so much, Zeresh thought, if my sister will look for solace in the bottom of a goblet.

———•———

When she woke the next morning, the house was quiet. Too quiet. She didn't hear her sons shouting as they exercised outside before starting their studies. The servants attended to her silently but wouldn't look her in the eye. They tried to guess what she'd want before she could even name it. Something must have happened. But she couldn't figure out what it could have been.

It took her hours to track down her husband. Even he had been afraid to face her, but he finally confessed to having seen it all happen.

"The king tired of the dancing girls, their flesh warm

in the firelight, heavy in his hands," her husband reported. "He wanted to show us, all the nobles he'd gathered there, how strong his decree was. He was drunk. I've never seen a man take in so much wine in one night."

Zeresh began to grow impatient. Her husband could go on when he got going, his language getting more flowery the closer he came to the heart of a matter. What she wanted was to get to the point.

He went on. "'Bring in my wife,' he declared. We all froze. It was as if time stopped. 'Prepare my wife for an audience and bring her in,' he said again. 'You will all see what beauty accrues to a king.'"

Zeresh could imagine it; the masses of embarrassed and horrified men, each avoiding the eyes of his neighbor, as the king finally stepped over the bounds of decency.

"No one knew what to do," he continued. "But we were all thinking the same thing. Even he couldn't ask a high-born woman—the queen!—to be exposed to such a scene. Spilled wine and a naked woman on each man's lap. But not mine," he quickly added, "I would not touch them."

"Oh, shut up and get on with it." Zeresh had no patience for his simpering devotion. What man didn't take an occasional interest in some girl? That had nothing to do with marriage.

"But he's the king. He will have his way," her husband said. "One of the ministers went to the harem,
spoke to the chief eunuch, and quickly returned. We
got back to eating and drinking, as if nothing had
happened. It could be hours before she'd be ready. In
the meantime, maybe the king would doze off, or take
one of the young girls back to his rooms for the night,
and we would all be spared the spectacle of the queen,
your sister's humiliation.

"But it was not to be. Within minutes, the chief
eunuch himself came into the room, his face as gray as
the well of the firepit. 'She will not come,' I heard him
whisper to the chief minister.

"The king was incensed. For seven days, he had
eaten and drunk and fucked as if he were not just a son
of the Creator, but a god himself. When word got to
him, he turned as if suddenly sober. His whole body
stretched and reddened with rage. He stalked out of the
hall, the ministers tripping over themselves to follow,
like lapdogs beneath his heels.

"By daylight, she was gone. We were all sleeping off
our drinks when they took her. No one knows where
she's been sent. Somewhere in Susa, so far as I know.
But that's all I know."

Zeresh fell onto a couch. Her husband watched as
anger and fear played across her face. It took a few moments, but anger won out.

"What has she done? Couldn't she have averted her eyes? It's a woman's lot to face embarrassment at her husband's hand. That's a truth all wives know. Even the king's. Especially the king's."

"Surely, my dear, I do not shame you." His feelings were really wounded, his peacock pride punctured that easily.

"You will not last a week as chief advisor if you take offense so easily," she snapped.

She stood up, paced back and forth over the length of the carpet. Her sister's advice of the day before was no longer useful to her. One thing was clear. She couldn't give the king a few days to sleep off his hangover and come back to his senses. He'd discarded those along with her sister sometime during the night.

"You have to go him now. Today," she told her husband. "Our whole family will be under a cloud of suspicion because of her little show of independence. We've been forced to wait this long. Now we can save ourselves and take what's due to us all at once."

She looked her husband over, took a final accounting of his abilities. They would have to do. There were two possible outcomes of the day ahead of them: complete ruin or great power. He was their only hope.

"Offer him everything," she said. "Tell him you'll refill the treasury up to twice what the last minister gave him. Tell him you'll personally bankroll his personal guard for the next six months."

He blanched. "That much? It will ruin us."

She brushed off his concern. "I'll earn it back. This is the only way to save ourselves."

"And your sister?"

"Don't say a word about her. I'll look into it. But I won't see the other side of the palace threshold again."

"But I'll be vizier. You will go where you please."

Zeresh finally felt like she understood Vashti, who knew the mind of the king better than anyone. "He won't forgive that easily. Our money will buy you inside the gates. My blood will keep me out. He's been king for years. Have you learned nothing of him yet?"

"Only that he's a fool in love with wine and war."

"He may indeed love wine and war, but he's no fool. That's why you must go now. Immediately. There's no time to waste. His men may be marshalling to come round us all up at this moment."

———— ◆ ————

Zeresh didn't dare leave the grounds of her own home. All of Susa would have heard about her sister's fate by now. She would be jeered and hissed at by everyone, even those she had counted as her friends since childhood. No one could afford to be seen taking her side, even out of pity. Besides, she wouldn't give them the pleasure of seeing her brought down.

Bitterness at her own lot kept her from showing it, but she worried for her sister. A queen cannot simply disappear as if she never existed. She must have left a trail. Why, though, couldn't she wait to show her stubbornness? She knew, Zeresh thought. She knew how important this week is for us, and yet she would make her stand now.

As had often happened since childhood, Zeresh felt herself struggling to lift off the shade that her sister had thrown onto her. Never out of malice. She was sure of that. Vashti just never had to think things through. The accident of beauty had given her the privilege to act first and consider the consequences later.

It had finally been her destruction, and for that Zeresh wept. Her beautiful, headstrong sister, trapped in a story written by their father and her husband, the king, so long ago, now banished who knows where because she had dared try to write one line.

Zeresh allowed herself another minute's sorrow and then set to work. She may not have been able to go to the palace, to walk through its immaculate gardens, watch the fish swim golden beneath the surface of the ponds as the sun set across them, but she could bring the palace to her home.

Hours later, Hegai, the harem's chief eunuch, was led into her private office, his face a closed mask of sly wit.

She offered him her finest date wine, almonds picked from her own trees, cakes bursting with pistachios and cinnamon. She knew his weaknesses. His manhood may have been taken from him. His hunger never was.

"The king is most gracious and magnanimous," he answered, when she asked after his wellbeing.

"Because you're not dead or exiled, too, I suppose."

"My king sees fit to keep me in service."

"No one could have expected her to react that way. Not even so capable a head eunuch as you are. Surely our king, in his wisdom, has seen that."

"So it would seem."

"I am glad to see you, then, still in your proper place."

They danced around each other. But they were old hands at this kind of thing: sweets for the belly and the ear, and only then the truth.

"And have you lost any workers of late?" she asked

"Only one. Artakama, poor boy, has been assigned to a new task and moved away from the palace to serve my lord, the king, elsewhere."

They were getting to the meat of the issue.

"Has he had to travel far?"

"Happily for him, no. He gets the travel sickness, so it is his luck that he is to remain in Susa, although he is young and ambitious and will struggle at the restraints placed upon him."

"Surely, he must realize that his ambitions should be more modest now."

"He will have excellent guidance in that area, I'm sure."

"So, a teacher has been provided for him? One who understands the ways of the king and his kingdom?"

"The best I have ever seen. One so wise you would almost suspect any transgression would have been on purpose."

Zeresh could breathe freely now. For the first time since waking, she reached for nourishment and took a bite of one of the cakes set before them. Hegai was a good man and had always been an ally to her sister, but there was only so much he could say, even here in the privacy of her rooms. He had taken a risk coming to see her. That alone showed how little his love for her sister had dimmed.

She knew that his life depended on his allegiance to the king. She could ask for no more information than he had just given her. Vashti was alive. She was in Susa. The king had not abandoned her completely. That was enough to know for now. Even if her personal eunuch had been punished along with her, she had him, and with him, no doubt, a full household. Zeresh thought of the prison that would be her sister's life from now on, but she knew how Vashti felt about living in the palace harem. She imagined her sister, resplendent as always, laughing at Zeresh's naiveté for thinking her situation had changed one bit.

They talked of other matters. Hegai had already heard that her husband had gone to see the king, although the two men were still together when he slipped away to visit her. But the hour grew long, and he had to return. The women's building was no place to go missing from for too long. "They are too beautiful and too idle, and so they look for stories to tell each other and themselves," he said.

"Someone I know always said a woman's beauty was her curse."

"There is wisdom in that."

Which was the last they spoke of her sister, except as he passed her doorway to leave. They both knew that this would be the last they would see of one another. It's too bad, Zeresh thought. She liked Hegai. He knew how to have a conversation. He must have been thinking the same thing, because as he passed her in the doorway, he bent close and embraced her, the mask of aloofness briefly gone. "I will miss her," he whispered, which was, she knew, the truest thing he had said yet.

———— ◆ ————

By evening she knew that the king had taken her husband's money, that it had bought him the position of chief advisor. Within days, the king's anger passed, too, although she had no way of telling whether that was because of her husband's influence, or if it was the product of his new obsession. Women were being brought in from all over the empire to audition for the position of new queen. Not all were noble-born, as Vashti had been. Any girl young and plump with a round ass was welcome. Anyone who could catch the king's eye.

She took to calling her husband, "Your Excellency," at first in loving jest and then in earnest. He seemed to grow even rounder with power, his chest and stomach like a drum proclaiming his importance. Hangers-on scurried around her property whenever he was home. She had tables and couches set up in the courtyard once they had trampled the grass to powder.

She had been right about another thing: her husband's new position didn't buy her entry back onto the palace grounds. Her friends flocked back to her, now that she was married to the king's right-hand man, but she couldn't pass the palace's outer gate. She still had ways of getting the information she needed, though. She had been part of the grapevine for too long to be kept out now.

———— ◆ ————

Here it was, a year later, and very little had changed. They had traveled away from Susa and now back again. The good soil sprang beneath her feet. Her horse had traveled the road between her home and the palace so often in the past that it took her there almost without guidance. But she dismounted well away from the back gate, where Shaashgaz, too full of cynical mirth to care whether he was seen with her or not, came out to meet her.

He may not have been in charge of the harem, but he was obsequious enough to have wormed his way into the position of second in command. She was grateful for his time. She still had her properties—tenants, orchards, fields—to look after, and there were always her sons' needs. This one needed a new tutor, that one to be put in his place. But she missed court life, its glitter and secrets. She had no secrets now. His Excellency, her husband, kept his to himself.

And then there was the new queen. Shaashgaz told her himself. "Hegai took a liking to her, but between you and me, I can't tell why. Mousy little thing. Her cunt must be lined with hammered gold, though, because the king can't get enough of her. Calls her in three nights out of the week. Which I'll admit has put a glow in her cheeks that we had to work for months to get there with paints."

"Do I detect some jealousy? Did you have another

favorite?"

"Goodness, no. That's Hegai's business. I just take care of them after the king has used them up. But she's so common. No noble blood at all."

They had wound their way around the palace walls, which were as brilliantly white as ever. Thick ropes of ivy had been trained up the columns at even intervals. As always, people congregated around the main entrance to the outer court. Some waited for an audience with the king, others came to buy and sell from the ones with official business. Zeresh and Shaashgaz ignored them all, but she enjoyed seeing the mix of people from all over the empire—Babylonians, Egyptians, Macedonians—with their different styles of dress and hair, all mingling here at the center of it all.

"Perhaps he thinks she'll be more malleable than an aristocratic girl, who would come trailing a father and brothers who'd have ideas of their own," Zeresh suggested.

"Or maybe he just doesn't care about tradition. The empire is secure. There are no deposed kings' daughters to be fucked into submission."

"And will she?"

"Will she what?" He had lost track of the conversation, which often happened when he got going about the women he oversaw.

"She will be more malleable," Zeresh said, sure it was

true. "More than my sister ever was. She'll have to be. She knows nothing of how the palace works."

"I wouldn't be so sure. She's quiet. Keeps her thoughts to herself. Like your sister. Those are often the ones to watch out for. She's been helped along, of course."

This was news to Zeresh. Who was this girl who seemed to rise out of the soil?

"Someone's bought Hegai's preference?"

"Oh, come. You of all people know how things work in the palace. We all have to get by."

"Everyone except the king."

"Perhaps that's why he's the only one who doesn't know."

"Doesn't know what?" Zeresh thrilled at moments like these, when she felt a curtain was being pulled back, and she was allowed to see past into the dim corners.

Shaashgaz pointed to a man standing just inside the outer gate. He was taller than most of the men there, and saber-thin.

"She's Mordechai's little 'ward'."

"That's Mordechai? The spy?"

Shaashgaz arched his eyebrow. Everyone either knew Mordechai the Jew or knew his reputation. He was the king's most ardent secret agent, ferreting out treason, sometimes when it wasn't even there.

"About a month after all the potential brides started entering the harem, Hegai began wearing a very large necklace that appeared as if milled, polished, and deposited by fairies who live in the ground. He's been fawning all over the new girl ever since it appeared."

"But what does he want? Mordechai, I mean. He can't possibly suspect the concubines of sedition."

She studied the man. He seemed to be watching everyone and paying attention to none of them at the same time. She couldn't even be sure that he hadn't seen her, even though they were separated by gates, and a crowd of people moved between them. What a skill to have perfected, to look without seeming to do so, Zeresh thought. She wished for it herself on occasion.

"He wants what we all want, of course. Power. This is the oddest conversation, my dear. I seem to be saying things you should already know."

After Shaashgaz had gone back into the palace and to his girls, Zeresh wondered at herself, too. She stood outside the palace walls, the closest she had been to the king in a year. The court had moved three times. The rains had come and gone. So had the summer heat. They were finally back in Susa's mild winter. But she was still on the outside. Since her husband had risen to his new position of prominence, she had been invited back into the fold of noble society. Every door except the palace's was opened to her now.

And yet she felt her distance more keenly. Her husband left at daybreak every day. He wanted to be the first advisor the king would see each morning. When he did come home, his chest was more puffed than usual. He'd even begun to emulate the king's dress, wore clothes shot through with gold and a massive turban on his head. People bowed and scraped at his feet. They knew he had the king's ear.

All except one man. It was all she heard about when her husband did come home. He fumed about the man's disrespect, how he looked down his nose at him, how impertinent he was even to the second most powerful man in Persia.

"It's outrageous. He's nothing, cannot even come further than the outer courtyard, and yet he remains insolent. Curls his lip at me."

"It can't be all that bad. He must be expendable. We can put our heads together to find a solution. Who is he?"

A look of disgust took hold of her husband's face, as if he had eaten meat that had gone rotten. "I will not deign to have his name spoken in my home. It doesn't matter who he is. He must be cut down to size. I am the chief advisor to the king. He will bow to me in the end."

She could see that he was working himself up. But his anger worried her. It would cloud his judgment, and they needed him to be sharp.

"You have to let this go. It's not healthy to fixate on one man. You're getting careless. You may be the king's right-hand man now, but we can't be too careful. Some-one else can come along at any moment and offer him more gold. And then where will we be?"

The air seemed to go out of him. He deflated as only a fat man can, his spine burdened under all his flesh and the weight of his extravagant hat. "I cannot touch him."

"Silly man. I may be kept out of the palace, but even I know that the king is ignorant of what happens in his own courtyard. He's far too taken with all his new women. Surely, you can figure something out. After this problem of the nameless man has been taken care of, you can get back to worrying about the important things again."

It wasn't an affair of state, this obsession of his, but she was grateful that he still turned to her when something touched him this deeply. She didn't expect him to take her so seriously, though. For days, she saw him even less than usual. He was holed up with his own spies. Until the day he returned home triumphant.

"I've fixed that man now. In a month's time, he won't be a problem anymore."

———— ◆ ————

Her husband had asked her to dine with him, alone on the patio next to her rooms. A light dinner of fruit and pastries filled with goat and pheasant lay before them.

The last of the sun's warmth touched her back. She was filled with meat and cheese. He had ordered their richest wine to be brought.

He was crowing, showing off his skill for her. After all these years, she thought, he still wants to impress me. Before even hearing the details, Zeresh felt a burst of pride. He was finally growing into the power that had been placed into his hands. This was a man worthy of the title husband. And chief advisor, of course.

"These days of petitions bore the king. The workings of an empire can be so tiresome. It's far more fun to plan a campaign against rebellious factions. Well, the Afghan mountains have erupted again. The tribes there get restless," he said.

"But all the king asks is what's due a protector," he continued. "It's not much, just some money and conscripts. What young man wouldn't want to be in service to the greatest army the world has ever known? The king was riled up. He loves nothing so much as the thought of a military campaign. We talked for an hour. I advised him on strategy, corrected him when he underestimated the number of conscripts we'd need. Reminded him, of course, about the difficulty of provisioning an army through the mountains."

How tiresome he can be, she thought, even now, in his triumph. Zeresh cared nothing of the movements of troops. Talking to her husband sometimes made her wish for the conversation of her sister or Hegai. But she bit her tongue. Let him wend his way through this preamble. He deserved this chance to boast, after all. Not many men would live to say they had advised a king.

"I arranged to have that discussion followed by one about a road building project. Just the thought of it made the king's eyes wander to his wine bearer. Once he had a cup in his hand, I mentioned that another clan has been disloyal, only they aren't in the mountains, but have infiltrated our cities. Destroying them would be a morale-booster for the soldiers before the long trek into the Kush."

Her husband sat back, enjoying the memory of his own cleverness. Zeresh had to admire his cunning. Perhaps he is well suited to this after all, she thought. Though the sun had set and the servants were lighting small fires around the patio, she felt herself growing warmer, excited by what she was hearing.

"The king, in his wisdom, agreed that seditious forces need to be rooted out wherever they appear. Of course, I offered to pay for the entire operation. By month's end, that man," he spat, "who would sneer at me, and his entire clan, down to every woman and child, will be gone."

What power he has, she thought. She looked at him as if for the first time in years, how square his jaw still was under his beard, how strong his hands remained.

They had this home together, sons that they were raising, a shared vision of what their life could be, but she hadn't felt those hands on her skin in a long time. She hadn't wanted them. Until now.

Zeresh waited until the last torch was lit, then sent the servants away. She wanted him to herself. Just the two of them, joined together as they'd been for so long. She stood up, looked down at her husband, dropped her robes off her shoulders, and lowered herself into his waiting lap.

———◆———

It was only when they woke up the next morning that she learned that he'd kept the most important bit of news from her.

"I'm to dine with the queen tonight." He said it almost casually, as if to fool her into thinking this were an everyday occasion, that he was already used to intimate evenings with royalty. But the edge of self-importance in his voice gave him away. He has left me behind, she realized.

"It's to be me, her, and the king. So I must take care to dress well today."

"You've proven yourself to them all," she said.

"Yes, they turn to me for all manner of things now."

She called the servants, prepared his oils and perfumes

herself, watched as he wrapped himself in his finest silks. And then she watched him go.

———•———

The day stretched, interminable. The summer was coming. She could feel the air drying out already. There was so much to do before they'd be ready to leave for Persepolis again. She used the time between her husband's exit and the late hour when he would return to begin packing up the house, but the servants seemed sluggish all day. She had to prod and shout to get anything accomplished.

After a morning of frustration, the servants moving slowly, tenants coming to her with petty complaints, and her sons getting underfoot everywhere she turned, the gates opened, and Shaashgaz, her old friend, rode in, resplendent in his silks. Even his horse and litter were ornamented. Green silk threads winked from the fabric of his tunic and saddle.

"What a surprise, my friend," she said. His visit was not entirely welcome. There was too much to do, and too much to worry about. She kept checking the sun, factoring how long it would be before her husband sat down with the new queen.

"We weren't expecting you. I'm afraid my people are entirely useless today. They haven't yet prepared lunch." She couldn't simply ignore the social niceties, though. "And I won't hear of you not sitting down to eat with me."

"Have you lost your touch, my dear?" he asked, gently teasing her. "I thought you scared them all into perfect behavior."

With anyone else, she would take offence. He really was too impertinent, but his eyes laughed as he said it, and he hooked his arm through hers as soon as he was helped down off his horse. "No matter," he said, "let's walk around your lovely gardens. Everyone says that you've outdone yourself this year, that they are second only to the palace's."

How does he do it? she wondered. She knew his words were covering something, that there was method in his empty flattery, and yet all the agitation left her body. She surrendered to him, let him lead her farther into her own grounds. They followed the wall to the back of the property. The trees shaded them, birds of paradise rose in flocks against the walls.

"Oh, it is marvelous in here," he said. "It's a wonder how you managed to grow these climbing plums so tall and lush. What a gift it must be to cultivate your own grounds and family. You must be so proud of all that you've built."

"We've been lucky this year. The ground has been generous."

"And how are your boys? Growing as well as your flowers, I hope."

Where is this heading? she wanted to know. He wouldn't have arrived unannounced to ask after flowers and children, but she played along until he was ready to speak freely. "They do well. Our oldest is, of course, a great help to his father now that he has so many responsibilities. We're quite proud."

"About that." The tone of his voice suddenly changed. His usual arch lilt dropped away. His voice was still high, making him sound like the boy he was when his manhood was taken from him, but she only now realized how carefully he had constructed that mask of friendly gossip, that he was more than a canny court survivor. There was a serious man under all that ornamentation.

"There's been an incident at court. As you know, the king gets strange ideas in his head sometimes, which is what happened this morning. He woke up agitated about something, called for one of his advisors. Your husband was there early, as usual. When the king saw him, he ordered your husband to lead Mordechai the Spy through the streets of the market, proclaiming to all who could hear how loyal and good a servant he is. Your husband had no choice but to do it. He wore out his voice with shouting, but he looked like he wanted to kill the man the whole time."

"What? Is his chief advisor to be treated like a groomsman?"

"This is not the time to be offended."

She had pulled away from him, her anger flaring.

"How can I not? Is this how the king would treat the man who sits at his right hand, who practically bankrolled his government?"

"Aren't you frightened?"

"Frightened?" This stopped her. "Why should the wife of the most important advisor to the king be frightened when her husband is debased by a dissolute and foolish king?"

"Because it's Mordechai the Spy, of course."

"Who is he to me? Just another hanger-on at court, one of the men who lurk about looking for people to denounce or prove their loyalty."

"You don't know. The Creator help you, you don't know."

Shaashgaz looked genuinely upset. The mask pulled back even farther. How had she missed the fact that he was more than someone to idle away the odd afternoon with. This was the face of a true friend.

"Mordechai is the man your husband has plotted to kill. It's been the talk of the palace."

Zeresh was too shocked to speak.

"I thought your husband confided in you, that you knew his dealings."

"He does. He did. He used to. But he wouldn't let anyone utter the man's name in his presence. How was I to know? I've been banned from the palace. And my husband never mentioned Mordechai's connection to the queen. Is it possible he was the only person in Susa who doesn't know about it?"

"Only him. And the king."

Zeresh understood the implications of what he was telling her at once. "We are doomed." She knew this court better than almost anyone. "And he's to dine with the king and queen tonight."

Suddenly, she was very scared. The queen would expose her husband, she was sure of it. It's what she would have done had their places been reversed. The chain of events was as clear to her as if she was in the room. Her husband would swagger in, full of his own importance at being invited to eat privately with the king and queen. The queen would announce his treachery, and the king, besotted with her, would fly into a rage.

What would happen after was too horrible to con-template.

"Is there any hope for us?" she asked. Maybe Sha-ashgaz, this good man, could see a way out that she couldn't.

"It's hard to predict the king's moods. But if your husband throws himself on his mercy, perhaps you can all be saved."

Zeresh had to act. Forgetting her guest and what she owed him as a host, she ran to the stables.

"Saddle all the horses," she said to the first man she saw. "As quickly as you can. For my sons." Without waiting to see if he obeyed, she ran back to the house.

Her boys were still inside, innocent of what was about to befall them. She could hear them through the windows. High-spirited, but cruel in the way only children can be. One had grabbed his tutor's scroll, was tormenting the man. As she got closer, she saw the others point and laugh at him. They are so young, she saw, so assured of their place in the world.

She was about to call out to them, to tell them to leave their play and get ready to ride away, but its pointlessness hit her as hard as if a man had struck her across the face. Where would she send them? Not to their house in Persepolis. They would be found there. All she knew was court life. All her friends and distant cousins were connected to it. Anyone who might assist them was part of this world, too. There was no one to help them. And there were spies everywhere. All she could hope for now was what was left of her husband's good sense and the king's mercy.

And she, trapped here in her beautiful home, could do nothing about it. Events would unfold without her. They would swirl and settle, and then she would do what she had always done. She would find a way. But she didn't expect what came. Who could?

———————◆———————

That was what she wondered as she sat in her garden as Artakama, her sister's favorite—and only—eunuch, directed the servants who would no longer be in her service after today, though she could see the pity in their eyes when she lifted her head. The same question went round her head ceaselessly. How could I have predicted this?

Mostly, she stared at the soil. Only yesterday, her sons' feet had pounded it, one after another, chasing each other through the gardens. Now, the only sound was of the dampened whisper of servants moving around. Every so often, a maid sobbed and then ran into a far courtyard so she wouldn't disturb her mistress.

Zeresh felt the activity around her. She heard as if from a distance as Artakama directed her headman what to dispose of before the new owner took possession and told her women to pack for Zeresh. "Just clothes and linens. Leave the fine silks behind."

"Madam, we must go," he said to her after the work had been done. She could hear the kindness in his voice. He has grown used to being kind to broken women, she thought, but she didn't thank him for it.

Her throat had closed around all words. She doubted it would ever open again.

"I have sent your things ahead," he continued. "But we must go."

She didn't look up. She didn't acknowledge where she was or that he was standing beside her. He looked to the servants for guidance, but they had never seen her immobilized like this before, either.

Eventually, she knew, she would have to stand up. She would have to take a few steps, and then a few steps more, but she didn't know how to tell him that.

Instead, he cupped her elbow, his touch gentle but sure. So this is what my sister meant about the eunuchs' hands, she thought. Not pleasure, but safety. She had never, she realized, been touched like this, not by her father or her husband. Not even her sons' soft hands, since she passed them along to wet nurses as soon as they were born. She regretted everything, but maybe that most of all, the line of nurses and tutors who had known her boys better than she had. She had been so focused on their father, on what she could make of him, thinking she was setting them up well for a good future, each in his turn.

Artakama's hand stayed on her elbow, the other guided her back.

"Mordechai's men will be here to claim the house soon, Madam."

"They've taken everything from me," she finally said.

"You have me now."

And he led her, slowly, as tender as ever, to the gate, where a litter more magnificent than she had ever ridden in stood waiting, curtains open, inviting as the womb. He helped her in and then pulled the curtains shut. It was dark and warm. She thought she would like to stay in there forever, her cheek against the silk, her finger tracing the threads in the fabric. It would take a lifetime to move over the entire expanse, one silken thread at a time. She could start with the reds, then move to orange, blue, and green. She'd save the yellow that fringed the curtains for last, end with something to remind her of the sun.

Even as she thought it, she felt the litter begin to move, heard the gates pull back. Changing her mind, she reached for the curtain. She would look at her home one more time while it was still hers, but Artakama's hand clamped down on hers from outside, rougher now than before.

"You can't look at it, Madam. It's just a house now."

He gave the order to move, and protected her from seeing the head of each of her sons, spiked through and planted in the ground.

———◆———

They didn't travel far. Clever punishment, she thought, to house her sister here, so close to those who cared for her and then keep her locked away. When the gates, made of thick but unornamented wood, opened she saw how much larger the grounds were than they seemed from outside.

It was a comfortable prison, though she saw little of it in those first, terrible days. The sound of her sons' screams still echoed in her head, the feel of her youngest being pulled from her, his boy-soft skin still hot against hers, never left her. She stayed in her room, allowed Vashti to spoon broth into her mouth and stroke her hair.

She wished for death, but no one would kill her. She wanted to run into another life. When she finally rose, she ran to the compound's walls, walked their boundary over and over, imagined the life that was passing outside. She heard the thud of horses' hooves, and the slower plod of slaves' feet.

Soon the sounds died down, too. Susa grew silent. She thought they must be the only people left in the world, until Vashti reminded her that the court had probably moved on to Persepolis. "The summer will come soon, sister. You have never known such heat. We will see it through."

# CITY OF REFUGE

*"Most blessed of women be Yael,*
*Wife of Heber the Kenite,*
*Most blessed of women in tents.*
*He asked for water, she offered milk;*
*In a princely bowl she brought him curds.*
*Her [left] hand reached for the tent pin,*
*Her right for the workmen's hammer.*
*She struck Sisera, crushed his head,*
*Smashed and pierced his temple.*
*At her feet he sank, lay outstretched,*
*At her feet he sank, lay still;*
*Where he sank, there he lay—destroyed."*
Judges 5:24-27

———— ♦ ————

This is the sin of the city-dweller," her father taught. "To dig stone out of the ground and build a house. Such permanence leads to nothing but problems. First the house, then the neighbor who wants to take it from you, then the wall to protect it from that same man."

Yael sat at her father's feet with her brothers, sisters, cousins, all the children of the caravan. She was entranced by him, the thick braids that fell like ropes around his thin face, the passion that filled him when he taught them the lessons of their people.

"Remember this. We live in tents so we live free. We make no claim to any plot of land. The entire desert is open to us, and we go where we please.

"We were here before they arrived," he continued, "and we will be here when they all pass away from the earth. We make peace wherever we pitch our tents. The desert was ours before these people came, but they have built cities, while we remain in tents. They claimed the land, and we still roam."

The caravan had passed through this land every year of Yael's brief life. The men pitched their tents on the great plain between two walled cities. Her father found a lesson in each place they stayed, pointed to the cities, the fields, and showed the children what their gods demanded of them.

"We Kenites will always be welcome. City dwellers have no time to learn the old trades, to stoke the fires, hammer the bronze and iron. So long as we make their pots and the tools to drag through the ground behind their oxen, we will go where we please."

There was only one law they must not break, he

warned. "Never make a sword for an outsider. It is as my father taught me and his father taught him."

He lifted the scarab ornament that hung from a cord around his neck to show the children. Curved and intricately carved, it mimicked the pendants every adult around her put on at twelve years old as a sign of adulthood. Yael counted the years in her head until she received her own. It would be smaller, more delicate than her father's, more fit for a woman, but like his it would be holy and symbolic.

"We wear these to remind us of our duty to the gods, our pledge to live in peace with those around us. We must never raise our hands against another man. We must never make war with him."

Yael grew up with the security of the treaty makers. Just as her father promised, her family's caravan was welcome wherever it went. Agreements were made with all the leaders they encountered. The Kenites pitched their tents in exchange for the metalwork they provided. They stayed out of the skirmishes that surrounded them, watched as Israelites made war with Ammonites, and Ammonites went into battle with Philistines, who in turn fought the Moabites.

All around them, men struggled to take what the other had. Yael felt nothing of it. She grew up in a chrysalis of peace, her people's traditions as steady as the change in season. They moved, made peace, crossed paths with other Kenite caravans with whom they sang their songs to the gods. Before they set off in opposite directions, the young men switched places so they could learn a trade and find wives.

Heber had come as an apprentice to her father. Yael's mother had sat with the women of the neighboring caravan, investigated his lineage even as she already knew he was a cousin, as were all Kenites, then welcomed him into their extended family. Heber worked in her father's shop for two years, sanding pieces of bronze into perfect ovals, rectangles, squares until his fingers calloused and his wrists hardened with muscle. Only then did her father allow him to approach the fire. It was then he taught Heber how to fan the flames, to smelt the iron from the ore. He placed a hammer into Heber's hand and guided it along the metal.

By then, Yael had taken Heber to the caves that dotted the Judean hills. Once she received her pendant, she was freer to roam away from the tents. She had found the caves when they first arrived on the plain, then brought him into the cool semi-darkness where she kissed the cords of his neck, his jawbone, his mouth.

After he forged his first dagger, Heber went to her mother to ask permission to marry. Her mother sniffed, as all mothers do, and pretended to be offended by the thought of joining her precious daughter to this unworthy man.

She sent him away, as all mothers did.

He came back, presented her with seed cakes, washed her feet, asked again. She sent him away. Outside the tent flap, he laughed with Yael about their people's ritual of courtship.

The third time, her mother looked him up and down. She sighed, as if still troubled. "You'll have to do," she said, then rose from her cushion and embraced Heber, whom she had loved as a son from the moment he joined their tents, whom she had pushed Yael to notice from the start. She had encouraged him to dance, even when he was new and shy around the older men. She pointed out his shapely legs and broad shoulders, then found ways to allow Yael to sneak away with him.

Yael's life had gone as planned. Her father had hung her pendant around her neck on her twelfth birthday. At fifteen, the women of the caravan piled her black braids onto her head, crushed gemstones to powder to redden her lips, cheeks, and forehead. One year later, she married. By the time her thirtieth year came, she had a husband respected by his neighbors, a tent of her own, and children clinging to her thighs. Until Heber pulled back the tent flap at the end of a long day. "We have to leave," he said. "They're going to kill me."

The baby Yael was rocking to sleep jerked awake in her arms at the gruff sound of his voice and began to cry. She shushed her down, but looked up at her husband. He was nothing like the timid boy she had first loved. The years had not been kind to him. He'd grown anxious about the future and impatient for success. He'd been one of the first to scorn the old ways and take orders for weapons of all kinds once her father's generation began to die off or became too old to work, or to object.

"It's not our way," Yael had pleaded when she first saw the swords and spearheads he had forged cooling in the yard. But he had brushed off her concerns. "Those are superstitions and old wives tales. The world is opening to us. We will grow richer than any of our parents could have imagined."

"Nomads have no use for wealth," she said. "We have enough to fill our tents. It is better for us to be righteous than rich."

But it was as Heber said. In defying their ancestors' warning and breaking their bonds with the gods, they had prospered. Business grew brisker than ever. Everyone rejoiced at their newfound wealth, so Yael hid her uneasiness about her people's work. She watched as they made the instruments of war but still tried to live in peace with their neighbors. The echo of iron beaten into swords resounded all around them.

But when the Judean ended up dead on Heber's shop floor, Yael had not been totally surprised. What else is a sword built for except to kill, she wondered, despair pulling her stomach and shoulders down toward the ground. Could it be counted an accident when the man complained about his weapon's quality and ended up sliced through?

She wondered what the man had thought, coming in to inspect the sword he had ordered. She believed Heber when he said it was an accident. At least, she tried to believe him. The fragile bonds of treaty between the caravan and their settled neighbors depended on it.

After the first moments of panic subsided, the men of the caravan went into Beersheva, the closest town, brought back the city elders, and showed them the body, the wound across his stomach and arm. They looked to one another, doubt moving from one face to the next as if passed by hand. The people of the caravan watched anxiously as the Judeans closed into a tight knot, conferred with one another.

"You have been an honored neighbor to us," they said when they turned back. "We have all benefitted from your presence here, and we thank you for bringing this unfortunate event to our attention." It was best, everyone agreed, to proclaim the death an unfortunate mishap. Heber would leave, they decided, to keep the peace and appease the dead man's family. Judean justice held out some hope for him.

"There is a city of refuge, Kedesh, in the north," the elders said. "Go there. You can pitch your tents outside the city wall and still remain safe from the family's vengeance. No one can touch you so long as you stay there."

———— ◆ ————

"Everyone needs a metalsmith," Heber said by way of apology as Yael packed up their entire life. She resented him, but he was her husband, the father of her children, and every so often, she still thought she could see traces of the boy he had been, who had let her lead him into the cool shelter of a Judean cave. And so she loaded up all she owned: tents, rugs, textiles, deep bronze pots, and left the desert behind.

Now she walked among the people of Kedesh, each of whom may have spilled human blood, each an accident. No one spoke of past crimes here, but it never left her mind that she lived among killers.

Those who were burdened with blood guilt carried their misdeeds within their hearts, just as Heber did. The two of them never spoke of the man on the floor, his mouth open in motionless surprise, which is how he left this world.

Yael was lonely for her family here in the leafy north. Still, she had harbored a secret hope that they would find a more peaceful existence once they arrived in their new home. In her younger years, Yael had wondered if the desert caused men to lose their minds, pushed them

into the frenzy of greed and war. But it was the same
everywhere. Here, the winds didn't roll in off the desert,
bringing sand and heat, but from the shore of the sea.
The breeze was gentler, mixed the scent of conifer with
the distant brine, and yet the people to the east and
west gave their battle cries and ran back to fight time
and again, plundering and being plundered in turn.
The wars came as regular as the spring.

She tried to live the Kenite way, even in this place
where the lemony smell of peonies filled her mornings.
She taught her children the ways of their people,
pointed to Heber, who was welcomed by Israelite and
Canaanite alike. And though he defied the gods and his
heritage at the forge, he followed the Kenite tradition
and made treaties of peace with all his neighbors, even
with Sisera, general of the city to the east, who led a
warlike people, even more ferocious than the Judeans
she had known. There was no justice for his people that
did not come at the end of a sword, but her family, she
explained to her children, would remain untouched by
the violence of the city-dwellers. "Let them fight each
other," she said, her children sitting at her feet. "Our
gods have taught us another way."

The family, separated from a caravan for the first
time in Yael's life, settled in their new place, the tents
secured to the ground. Heber dug a well in front of her
tent flap. Yael marveled that she would not have to walk

to gather water or wood, but worried that the branches that lay so abundant on the ground would stay too wet to make a decent fire.

What she could not get used to was the view outside. Every morning, Yael woke to air unchoked by dust. When she stepped out of the tent, blue sky met deep green hills in every direction. The roads she walked were lined with cedars, their branches reaching above her to touch one another, driving her deeper into forested darkness before releasing her outside the city wall, where cyclamens ran riot along the base of the stone.

And when she passed through the city gates with the vessels Heber made stacked and balanced on her head, the women praised his Kenite mastery and bought her market wares.

Despite the novelty, she suffered long hours of solitude, which would have been filled with chatter and laughter in her caravan days. At those moments, Yael sent her thoughts south, wondered about her mother, sisters, brothers, all the cousins who walked between tents, their embroidered hems swinging along the ground, the children who ran wild until pulled back to order with a sharp call.

She missed seeing them, missed having her hair braided around her head by the other women, their hands tugging to pull the strands straight. She missed the feeling of her own hands in another woman's hair.

From this distance, she watched in her mind as they gathered to cook and sing. She watched the men dance in reverence to the gods, their arms raised high above their heads, while the women sent their voices up into the heavens.

Yael never stopped missing her people, but in time she began to enjoy the north, how the trees absorbed the sound of her passage, unlike the rocky mountains, which echoed her footfalls back to her. Soon enough, though, the world's tension flared.

Sisera, always ready for a fight, led his people out into the broad valley. The people of Kedesh followed his army to see what would unfold. They brought jugs of wine and water, rounds of tightly wrapped cheese and soft bread in preparation for the spectacle to come.

Yael joined them. She walked as far as the crest of the mountain. Across the way, she saw a woman among the soldiers, her arms raised to the sky. Her men massed behind her, ready to battle, but no one moved until, in a single swoop, the woman dropped her arms and released them. The men coursed down the hillsides, ran over the dark earth that was better suited to growing than cutting down. When the two armies collided, the onlookers couldn't tell who was fighting whom, where one side ended and the other began.

Yael heard the screams of the wounded, the cries of the dying. They begged their gods to spare them. She had never been this close to such carnage. Before the first wave of men had fallen, she left the crowd of onlookers, turned back for Kedesh. When she reached her tent, she went directly to the well, pulled up jar after jar of water, and scrubbed every part of herself clean, as if enough water could rid her of the bloody images she had just seen.

Even after the ground was soaked with water, even after she had rubbed the skin raw on her arms and cheeks, Yael still had a sense that nothing was as it should be.

The trees did their work. They tamped the sounds beyond and below them so that she could no longer hear the battle that raged down the road. She watched their branches bend and straighten in the wind. The only sound she heard was the chirrup of a bird somewhere high above her head.

It distressed her. Yael wasn't used to silence. She wasn't used to being alone, but the paths around her tents that led in and out of the city lay empty. Everyone was there on the ridge watching men throw themselves at death. She didn't know how to fill her time without the simmer of chores, the comfort of work.

She walked slowly around the largest tent, looking for rips to sew, but didn't find any. She checked the fire pit, where she kept the embers smoldering in preparation of the next meal. They glowed, as predictable and orange as dawn. She counted the copper pots she had already counted that morning, then stacked them again. They were ready to be carried to the market, which sat empty now of everyone except the very old or infirm who couldn't make the walk to view the battlefield. Finally, she went into the enclosure where they kept their animals, lured the goats to her with handfuls of fresh hay, and milked the females one at a time, until she had filled a jug with the steaming milk.

Yael let the milk stand for a few minutes, until it developed a layer of cream that she skimmed off the top to feed to her children for dinner. She was still there, hidden from the road but able to see it, when she caught sight of a man running toward her through the trees. He was alone, and kept turning his head over his shoulder, as if to watch for someone following him. By the time he reached her tents, he could barely move. He ran through the property as if he had a particular destination, as if he was looking for something. When he found her, he bent over, his hands clutching the sides of his waist, his elbows flared to either side as his chest heaved. Yael watched as his back surged up and down with each breath he sucked in and let out.

He was looking for me, she realized, although she couldn't understand why. She didn't recognize him, although he had come to her home. He was clothed for war, his breastplate still tied around him, but he was a small man, shorter than many women, with stringy muscles running up his arms and legs.

It was only when he stood back up that she saw the cuffs he wore around his wrists. She recognized them immediately. Heber had forged them. He'd been paid handsomely. And why not? A general can afford to adorn himself with the best workmanship, the priciest metals.

That was how she knew the man. The bronze that gripped Sisera's arms shone pink from the alloys Heber had mixed in. The metal was hammered as thin as a leaf hanging from a tree. Any seams between the plates were polished so smooth they were invisible. She could make out the designs on each, still as clear as the day Heber finished them. On the right arm, a king being served by a stag who stood upright on two legs. On the left, a man under a tree, its canopy a series of circles within circles that wound all the way around Sisera's surprisingly delicate wrist.

"Give me some water," he said. "I have run far to reach a friendly place. My enemies surround me. They pursue me. Please, give me some water."

Yael's hair still held the moisture from the water she had showered over herself. Here was the man who was the cause of her revulsion asking for water to sate and cleanse himself, as she had tried to clean herself of him. Heber had made his peace with Sisera, but to Yael, who still held by the old ways, who grieved at each sword that came out of her husband's shop, he was the living image of how far her people had fallen.

They were all barbarians to her, the Canaanites, the Judeans, the Arameans; all would trample what the gods had made to claim a slightly bigger piece of it. Sisera was the worst of them all. Yet here he stood, above her but at her mercy. He could not drink unless she drew the water for him. Yael looked down. At her feet lay the jugs of milk and cream that she had just separated.

In that moment, Yael saw the choice that had just been given to her. The future of two nations had been placed in her hands. The Canaanites had already lost the battle. Sisera wouldn't be here if they hadn't. He was the only thing that stood between more bloodshed and peace. If he died, the fighting would stop.

Yael recoiled from the thoughts that were forming in her head. She was a Kenite, she reminded herself. She could not lift her hand in violence against another person. But no matter how she tried to deny it, she had watched as aggression had been used to resolve disputes all her life. She understood its logic. She weighed out her choices. One death, of this man who had brought destruction to so many, against the countless others that would follow if Sisera were allowed to leave her home. She was torn. She had to decide.

Yael looked up at the general. She rose to her feet,

gestured toward the ground. "Drink this cream instead. It will serve you better than water."

She led Sisera out from among the goats and into the tent. "Thank you," he said, as humble as a roadside beggar. Yael couldn't swallow. The spit stuck in her throat, but her hands around the neck of the jug didn't tremble.

She set the jug down, spread out the thickest skins she had. Sisera sank down onto them like a man saved. Yael watched her arms as they stretched toward him. She watched as his hands rose to meet hers, felt their fingers graze as the jug passed from her to him.

Sisera raised the pitcher to his mouth, swallowed quickly, the lump in his throat bobbing up and down as the cream filled him. When the jug was empty, he reached out his hand. "Give me the milk, too." Yael ran outside, scooped up the second, heavier, jug. The milk splashed over its lip as she rushed back inside. Sisera grabbed it out of her hand, drank deeply, then lay back on the skins. His face had taken on some of the color that battle and retreat had robbed of it. Although he did not reach from one end of the skin to the other, he lay with his limbs spread wide. He was no longer a supplicant at her door. He was a general who expected to be obeyed.

"Thank you," he said, his voice relaxed. "Don't let anyone in. I have to rest, replenish my energy. Then I will go back and take my revenge on that woman, Deborah, on her general, and all the people who would fight me." Yael saw that he felt safe with her. She was just a woman whose husband had made a pact with him. She didn't carry a sword or spear. She would never go to battle. To a man like Sisera, who thought all men could be divided into those who fought for him and those who fought against him, the idea that a woman could harm him was unthinkable.

Yael was at war with herself. She wanted to be alone again. She wanted to cry and scream and tear at her hair. My whole life has led to this moment, she thought, and I don't know what to do.

Yael watched him grow sleepier. She kept herself coiled next to the tent flap, afraid to go too close to him. His smell, of sweat and vinegar and something bitter she couldn't identify but which she thought must be the vestiges of fear, radiated from him. It repulsed her. "Enough to kill him?" she asked herself. "Enough to go against every belief you hold?"

Sisera sighed. He had forgotten his cares, if only for the moment. She had to act quickly if she was to act at all. He would be deeply asleep in minutes. Yael didn't allow herself to think. She ran outside to where Heber had his forge set up, scanned the ground until she found a tent peg he'd made but had tossed aside, and his heavy hammer, whose strikes against metal made up the soundscape of her life. She gripped them tightly.

"Forgive me," she whispered up into the cedar canopy, where she imagined her father and every ancestor who preceded him perched, then reentered the tent, her hands behind her back. Sisera had curled onto his side while she was outside. He lay like a child, his knees drawn up, arms bent next to his head. He breathed evenly as she approached. She raised the peg above his temple, held it straight with her left hand. At the moment she swung the right hand over her head, he opened his eyes and comprehension lit them. He started to form a word, but Yael brought the hammer down with as much force as she could muster before he could finish it.

She felt the metal slip down. She felt how easily it cracked bone and slid into the soft matter within. Blood spurted up and onto her. She had hit the peg with so much force that it passed through his head, pinned his corpse to the ground.

When she saw that he was dead, Yael ran outside, bent over and threw up everything in her stomach.

She stayed there on the ground, afraid now of what she had done, afraid of the body whose blood even now stained the skins and leaked onto the rugs inside the tent. Her head filled with the sounds of crows, each releasing its harsh caw into the wind, churning in her ears above the sound of her father's voice, repeating, "We never raise our hands against another man." Now that the act was done, Yael didn't know how she would face her own children, whom she had berated every time they punched or kicked one another in the course of a childish argument. She had told them too many times to remember that they were desecrating the gods, defiling their family and people.

Her thoughts were so tangled that Yael didn't hear the footsteps of the men who ran toward her until they arrived in front of her. When she looked up, her face was splattered with blood, dirtied with tears. Her mouth was still wet with vomit.

"Sisera?" they asked. They still wore the mud of the battlefield on their legs and thighs. Each man's skin shone, his eyes glinted, focused and empty at the same time. They had left the valley, but the trance of war still held them. These were the enemies Sisera had run from, the Israelites for whom she had become a murderer.

Yael's throat closed again. It fought all language, so that all she could manage was a wave in the direction of the tent. One of the men lifted the tent flap and gave a shout of joy. He rushed back to his companions, his eyes glowing with admiration for the woman who sat shattered at their feet.

"We are saved!" he shouted. He pointed to one of the other men, said, "Run. Bring Deborah, bring the general, bring everyone. This woman has given us victory today!"

The men raised their voices, sang praises to their God, to Yael's beauty and her bravery. They cursed the memory of the Canaanite general, celebrated his gory end. Yael heard none of it. As the men flung themselves into the frenzy of triumph, she crawled away, hid in the enclosure with the goats. Their earthy smell, pebbled droppings littering the ground, were a reminder of what her life had been until she lifted the hammer above a man's head. She could never go back. Nothing would be as it was, even as the world itself didn't change.

———— ◆ ————

Noise filtered back to her from in front of the tent. Yael could hear Heber, the babble of her children, more male voices as they joined the men who had stayed to watch over Sisera's body, as if somehow the dead could stand up and sneak away. For the first time since they had come, Yael felt afraid. Heber had made a pact of peace with Sisera. He would be angry with her. She couldn't even imagine what he would do in that anger.

But it wasn't Heber who found her there, her forehead bent against the flank of a pregnant goat. Instead of his heavy tread, she heard the hiss of fabric as it swept along the ground.

"Get up," a woman commanded. Yael looked over

the goat's black and grey back. It was the woman from the battlefield, the leader of all the Israelites.

Deborah was the most striking woman Yael had ever seen. Iron grey hair bristled past her temples and neck. Her face was a quarry of etched lines and furrows, yet she did not look old. She looked like time did not touch her as it did the rest of them. Her lips were pressed firmly together. Her jaw pulsed. She was not used to being disobeyed.

They could hear the men singing. One by one and in small clusters, the men had gone to look at Sisera's body, his limbs as calm as in sleep, his head pierced and deformed, and came out with a story of what happened. Someone already began to compose verses in Yael's honor. When other voices joined him, Yael caught snatches of it,

> *Praise Deborah and Yael, greatest among women*
> *Mother of our nation, deliverer of our sons*

The sounds in Yael's head finally stilled. All the voices receded, the storm of wind quieted. The enclosure filled with the goats' bleating, her own heartbeat, and Deborah's firm presence.

"We came here for refuge," Yael said, as if Deborah could know her husband's history, the accident that sent them running to Kedesh. "I live here surrounded by killers, but I am the only murderer in the city."

She thought Deborah would understand her grief. She had heard of the older woman's wisdom, how she sat in the stillness of her God's presence to hear her people's complaints, then judged fairly between them. This woman, Yael was sure, would see how terrible it is to have taken another person's life, but Deborah grew impatient.

"Stand up, woman." Her tone was as unyielding as an avalanche of stone.

Deborah strode over to Yael, yanked her roughly to her feet.

"Do not become weak as all the other women now," she said. "It's too late for that."

"What of Sisera's family? His people? Will they come to take my life in revenge? Will they kill my husband, my children?"

"Sisera was a coward. He ran as his men died. Only his mother will weep for him. He has fouled his own memory among all men."

Yael marveled at Deborah's ferocity. She thought she would find a woman's softness, but Deborah was like everyone else in this cursed land. They all thought the only way to honor their gods came through someone else's destruction.

"You are a heroine to my people," Deborah said, as if faced with someone so simple she could not understand the basic ways of the world. "Listen to them. Your grand-children's grandchildren will remember your name."

Outside, the men continued to sing,

> *She did not waver, she did not delay,*
> *Her hand was steady, her heart was pure.*
> *She trampled over her enemy's body,*
> *Left him lifeless, attached to the ground.*

"They are getting it all wrong," she said. "I am not like you. I am not one of you." Still, Deborah ignored her. Even she could not see how her men were turning Yael into one of them, who thirsted for bloody victory. Yael felt the world spinning around her, sky becoming ground, ground where sky should be.

Deborah kept talking, "Come out and meet them. Let them see the woman who accomplished what they couldn't do."

Yael allowed Deborah to guide her out of the enclosure. The goats scrambled after them as they walked. Yael saw the back of her tent, the fabric's red and green dyes faded with time and exposure. The breeze pushed against it, barely ruffling the heavy material. It looked as it always did, solid and familiar. It gave no indication that the proof of her crime lay within.

When they came around the front, the men shouted. Night had fallen, and someone had lit a fire that sent

their shadows jumping as they waved their swords and
spears in the air above their heads. A few let loose shrieks
or frenzied war cries. Yael cringed at each sound. They
didn't belong here. A home was no place for battle. Too
late, she thought, for such fine distinctions. She had
brought the fight here herself.

Her younger children ran to her, clung to her
thighs and hands. In their faces she saw a mix of pride
and bewilderment. This was worse than everything.
Worse than disobeying her ancestors, defiling herself
with the blood of another man, she had betrayed her
children. She had gone against everything she had tried
to teach them. All those years of fighting against the
bloodthirsty ways of their neighbors, only to prove to
them that she was no better.

Her own death would be preferable to this, she
thought. "I shouldn't have done it," she muttered. "Let
them kill each other without me," but only Deborah
heard her. The older woman just snorted. "That's a fine
thought to have after you've already acted. Go ahead,
say something. It's not every day an army of men listen
to a woman speak."

Yael gathered herself. She had to find just the right
words to make this right again, to turn the tide back, to
make them see what she had meant, that her act should
lead to the end of war, not this crazed victory. She stood
behind the fire, her face lit from below, the solidity of

her body fading into the surrounding darkness.

"Put down your swords," she said. "Beat them down. Raise your hands in peace," but her voice was not loud enough to rise above the din. The men, who had left a valley where they had been prepared to die, could not stop their tumultuous revelry. They were possessed by it. They thanked their god, the ground, each other. They promised vengeance on all their enemies. They did not hear her.

She tried again, "Don't celebrate this death. Let it be the last."

No one paid any attention to her. She had already become the woman in their song, the one who didn't hesitate, who went after the same glory they chased. Nothing she said would change that. Yael felt trapped between reality and the myth they were constructing, between the tents and the road, the ground and the sky. In between, the tranquil cedars rose, unhearing, eternal.

# SHILOH

*"There was a man from Ramathaim of the
Zephites, in the hill country of Ephraim, whose
name was Elkanah son of Jeroham son of Elihu
son of Tohu son of Zuph, an Ephraimite.
He had two wives, one named Hannah and the
other named Penina; Penina had children,
but Hannah was childless."*
Samuel 1:1-2

———◆———

For as long as I remember, my father's wives had
agonized over me. They loved me, and so they
tried to hide their distress, but I had eyes to see
and ears to hear. I saw the shepherds at the well trace
the shape of other women's bodies as they passed, their

round hips swinging back and forth. I heard them discuss the finer points of one girl's poppy-red lips or another's hair that bubbled over her back like a ripe cluster of darkest grapes.

At those moments, I looked down at my body, my fingers pulled at the lank hair that clung to the contours of my narrow forehead and sharp cheekbones, or rose to my own thin mouth that I've been told stretches too wide across my face.

The problem was obvious. I was ugly in a region of women prized for their beauty, so I watched all the other young women be claimed as brides and ride off into homes of their own. As each left, I stayed behind and wondered if I would remain a burden to my father and brothers for the rest of my life.

My mothers tried to console me. "The men of this region know so little about women," they said, "but there are some who have the discernment to know that the way a woman looks promises nothing about her ability to bear him children," but it meant nothing. They knew as well as I that a girl's looks were the currency she used to attract a mate. I watched them worry over my fate like hens clucking together over fallen seeds.

Imagine, then, the excitement in our house when a man came to inquire about me. My mothers and I hid behind a door to watch as he spoke with my father. He was of middle age, older than I would have hoped for when I was younger, but I had accepted that whoever expressed interest in me wouldn't be one to make other women's hearts uneasy. His manners were fine when he ate and drank, but I got no more of an impression of him than that.

Later, the three of them brought back more information. "His name is Elkanah," the first said. "He is not a rich man, with only two servants, a few acres to his name, and a small flock of sheep."

"But he boasts a fine lineage that goes back generations, and counts leaders and wise men among his ancestors," said the second.

"And it is well known that he is pious and devoted to his first wife, though she has given him no children," said the third, who had given birth to me. Though she was my father's last wife, she entered a home and sisterhood with her fellow wives and was never treated as lesser than the others.

My father said yes, of course. Even a poor man is acceptable for an ugly daughter.

My mothers fussed over me in the days that followed. They prepared baths of milk so I would go to my husband with skin as soft as a newborn calf. They mixed pots of kohl and rimmed my eyes and made jars of perfumes that left me smelling like a field of wildflowers. They packed linen sheets and fine clay pots for me to take into my new home.

"Take these as gifts for Elkanah's first wife," my first mother said.

"The men can worry about bride price and dowry," said the second. "She is the one with whom you will share your life."

"You will find a husband and a sister at once, as we did so long ago," said the third. "She will become closer to you than your own heart."

I believed them. They were my mothers and had seen all manner of men and women, and had the wisdom of generations of mothers before them to pass along.

What they couldn't prepare me for was Elkanah's first wife's beauty. She was everything I was not. Her skin glowed like sand under the sun. Her hair was as dark and thick as the deep recesses of a cave. Her neck rose long and straight above delicately plump shoulders. She was a delight to behold. I thought maybe that was why she didn't open her arms to me, but my mothers had warned me of that. "First wives often don't welcome the second wife at first. After all, you are younger, and she has not had to share her husband with anyone until now.

"But wait. Things will work out. Who knows a woman better than another who shares the same man's bed?"

I believed them about that, too. They ran my father's household as one. All their children found refuge in any of their laps. The three of them spun around my father, the stars to his moon, but it was to each other that they were devoted. They shared the work of their lives, and loved one another for it.

———◆———

It wasn't to be that way for me. Childbearing came easily. Milk poured from my nipples and stained my dresses. My children quickly grew fat and content on it. Even before I weaned the first, I grew large with the second, and before I weaned the second, my womb was filled with the third.

And so it went. I grew round with the seasons. At each birth, I held the warm flesh of my newborn against my skin and felt a newfound pride in what I was capable of doing.

Still, Elkanah remained devoted to Hannah and did not come to love me.

I took solace in my children. I gathered them around me, inhaled their smells, the dirt, milk, and traces of rosemary they trailed behind them. I told myself they were enough. That they were ample compensation for what was missing. But my closeness with them was never going to last. Already my oldest were pulling away from my embraces. The boys turned their heads when I tried to kiss their cheeks, the girls walked with their heads together. I was left out of their childish confidences.

It is as it should be. It is the way of the world. A mother brings her children into life and then sets them on their way. They never could have been mine forever. My job, as Elkanah reminded me, was to push out children. "My little breeder," he called me, and then took the flesh of my hips into his hands, squeezed lightly, although there never was much to grab, even after so many pregnancies.

At those moments, my body bared to him, each fold of muscle and dimpled skin a mark of how much I had given him, I could almost pretend he spoke out of affection. But then he'd smack my rounded haunch and send me away. "Let's see how efficient we've been this time," he'd laugh, then wait until I told him I was with child again.

And they came, girl after boy after girl after boy. Every time the midwife came to cradle me as I screamed a new child into the world, I knew the only power I would ever have. My only saving grace. After it was over, I would hold the baby to my chest, peer into its unseeing eyes and whisper, "He may not love me, but I will do better for you."

So let the others snicker as I pass. Let them call me a cow, my udders always swollen and full to bursting, a new infant strapped to my chest, another to my back, and little ones tugging at my sides. Even here, where women walk sway-backed and big-bellied for most of their adult lives, I outshine the rest. But while the women laugh, the men commend me. They call me a credit to my husband.

They don't know what I do. They have never watched Elkanah take Hannah's hand in his, or kiss her palm. They have never seen him slide his fingers across her cheek or the way his eyes brighten when he catches sight of her. They have never heard the laughter that comes from his room when she spends the night with him.

I have lain awake, my children's breaths a warm cocoon, listening, not for the quickened breaths, the gasps, or moans, but to the hum of their voices in the dark. It is then I wonder what it would be like to have a man love me enough to talk to me, to open his mind to me, but I was not brought into his home for conversation. I was brought to give him what Hannah could not, and nothing else.

He doesn't treat me badly. Anyone watching would call him an exemplary husband. My children are cared for, even the girls and younger boys who will eventually leave to make their own way. He even shows me respect, of a kind. When we are not alone in his room, where his body shows its desire even if his heart does not, he makes sure I have grain to eat and wine to drink. "You must stay strong," he tells me. "Do not tire yourself out." It is all in the service of his growing family, but I take every sentence as a sign that he values me. If that doesn't add up to love, it is some small comfort.

I held out hope that that my mothers' words would bear fruit, that I would gain a sister in my marriage. I waited, quietly giving way to everything Hannah demanded, but after my third pregnancy, after the midwife had come and gone, and a baby's squealing cry filled the rooms and yards of our home again, she picked up Elkanah's name for me. "Breeder," she said, "your child has fallen. Go see to him." She was careful never to say it in our husband's hearing, so he never saw how it pained me, and because he never probed my mind, he didn't know how she had twisted the only bit of affection between my husband and me into a slur.

I was just a second wife. I couldn't even tell him not to share what happened between us—sparse as it was— with her. I couldn't tell him that I wanted something between us to be ours alone. Does a cow ask for privacy? Does it demand the secrecy of the bedroom?

And so the years passed. I ballooned with life, leaked it, fed it, my womb never empty for long, and grew used to my own silences. Even my mothers didn't listen.

"Do not tell us of the difficulties in your marriage," they said when I cried in those early years. "Do not invite anyone into your home life, not even us. You are a wife now. Your task does not begin and end in the bedroom. You must protect the boundaries of your household. In everything you do, you must remember your husband's good name. You must guard it as your own. It is yours now."

After that, if anyone asked why my cheeks were wet, I said that I had held a crying child to my face. At night, their gentle snores covered the sound of my sobs. I loved each of them. I relished the tangling of my limbs with theirs, the way they fit themselves into my shoulder or curled against the curve of my hip. I gave thanks for their untroubled sleep, their trust in my presence. But each night, I counted the days I had left with them, the nights they would lie with me. I dreaded the day that would surely come when my bed would be empty, and I would lie alone, night after night, while whispers came through the wall from my husband's bed.

Is it any wonder, then, that my sadness curdled into bitterness? Here I was, my body inhabited over and over again, each time a gift to Elkanah, and yet he still loved Hannah more. I hated myself for it, but I couldn't stop the tumor of resentment from growing inside me, another fetus I carried alongside the others. This one never left. It had no nine-months gestation, no birth or growth outside the confines of my body. It stayed there, mutating until it filled so much of me that it became me. I felt my lips grow even thinner into the grimace of the aggrieved. Only my children brought laughter out of me. Only they saw whatever was left of the girl I'd been when I entered Elkanah's house.

And still, it was Hannah's complaints I heard.
"Give me a child," she cried to Elkanah. "I am half a
woman." She glared at me. "Even Penina has surpassed
me." And always he smoothed her hair, shushed her as
if she were a child herself. "Don't cry," he said. "You are
all I need. I love you more than any child ever could."

He didn't understand, but I did. What was the use
of being born a woman, of the blood and cramps, the
monthly cycle of expectation, if it ended with nothing?
Within the depths of my heart, I agreed with her. She
was not a whole woman. No one ever asked me, so I
never shared my thoughts, and maybe I was the only
one to see it, but I came to know that together we made
a complete woman. I made the babies. She got his love.

She got the better part of the deal. My babies would
grow and leave me. My body would stop making them,
and I'd be left with nothing, just the memory of a time
when I was needed. She would be treasured forever.

The worst of it came when Elkanah packed us all
up—Hannah, me, the children—and took us off to
Shiloh to give his yearly sacrifice. The babies cried, the
children complained of boredom and aching feet, the
donkeys brayed out their protests. Their tails swatted
back and forth over their haunches in search of flies to
scatter. And all the way, Elkanah raised his hands to
heaven, sang his prayers, and tried to get the rest of us

to show some enthusiasm for our godly pilgrimage.

I was always too busy to sing. It fell to me to pack our food for the trip, to ration it out over the two days' walk, to rein the older boys back in when they ran off the road in search of lizards to poke or the carcasses of animals long or newly dead.

"Look, Mama," they said at least three times a day, and then brandished a bleached thigh bone or dead bird, its neck bent or twisted to the side. I was too tired to ask if they had found those small bodies or killed the birds themselves.

Hannah sat silently on her plodding ass. Always. Her head hung, her eyes cast down to the ground, she seemed to follow only the shadows as they told the story of our progress. What she didn't do is offer to help.

And every year, my hair thinned after so many pregnancies and escaping in sweaty tendrils from the cloth I'd draped over my head to protect me from the sun, I came down off my donkey to build a fire in the evening, feed every one of us, prepare the beds for all my children.

All the while, Hannah sat morosely to the side, Elkanah holding her hand lightly between his, whispering in her ear.

The children saw it all. He never accounted for that, but they knew how things were arranged in our household and punished me for it. Half the time, the boys ignored me. The girls looked back and forth between Hannah and me, clutched my wrists or handfuls of my dress in their fists, unsure if they should shield or despise me. I dreaded the day they would find the words to ask what was obvious to anyone with eyes to see.

"Will I be like her, Mama, or will I be like you? Will I be loved?"

Every year I wondered at other people's blindness. The priests saw Elkanah's piety, the flawless ewe he led into Shiloh and up to their waiting altar. They heard his psalms to the Lord and joined their voices to his and ignored the pain of his careworn wife.

Each year, the sacrifice was given, the meat cut off the bone, a portion for the priests, the rest for us. Elkanah watched carefully as the pieces were cut—one each for my children and me, a double portion for his beloved, his Hannah.

It had been years of this. Even as my brood grew and I increased our household with fine sons and healthy daughters, she found favor with him. "Look at me," I cried out, "a vineyard full to bursting, but you water that barren field even knowing it will give you nothing."

I couldn't help myself. I could no longer be silent. Here we were, in the most sacred of places, the Ark of the Lord as witness to our good fortune, to give thanks and pray for more. We brought the best we had to sacrifice, and in return we got so much, but not from Hannah. She had nothing to do with it. She couldn't produce a thing.

Then I became the villain when she pushed away her meal—her double portion of sustenance and love—because I said what was only true. Elkanah shot me a look filled with more than disapproval, more than disdain. There was loathing in his eyes as he followed her away from the hearth, even as I knew he would plow my body that very night to reap the rewards of his holy devotion all over again.

It was that look. The disgust, as if I, mother to all his children, meant nothing to him, that clasped my heart and shut my mouth for another year, but a woman can only watch as if from the sidelines of her own life for so long before her silence becomes more than the lack of sound. It becomes a muzzle as on a dangerous beast. Do not be surprised, then, if the animal lunges in attack when it is removed.

So it repeated. I grew heavy and gave birth. I worked. We went up to Shiloh. Hannah sat pitying herself, drawing attention to her own misery. I spoke.

"Elkanah," I said, more beseeching than in anger. "Have I not given you what every man desires? Look at all our children. Their faces are alight with life. See this one," and then held up the baby, still swaddled, only his face emerging from the cloth. "See how perfect he is. Everyone comments on the way his face blends the two of us in his one form. Why then do you withhold even affection from me?"

But Hannah had to be the center of attention. Even as I showed the world the contents of my heart, how it bent toward my husband though he pushed it away, she went through her routine, the one I had seen so many times before. She sighed, pushed her dish away, and rose to return to her bed. As always, Elkanah turned on me. "Can you not keep your mouth shut? It is because of you that she suffers."

I wanted to protest. "It is not my good fortune that closes her womb," but he had already run to catch up with her. They stopped there, enclosed in an embrace for all to see, while my daughters coiled themselves around me, as if to protect me from life itself.

Perhaps something snapped in her as it had in me, because she didn't lower her voice this time, didn't depend on his pity to bend his head in closer to hers so that he could hear every shuddered word.

"Don't you see how I suffer," she wailed. She flung her hand out in my direction, as if to mark and erase me in one gesture. "Even she is given children, but I remain childless."

"Hush," I heard Elkanah say. "My heart is bound up in yours. You know how I love you. Come now," he held her face between his fingers. My own cheeks ached from never having felt that kind of touch. "My love is better than a son, better than ten sons. It is yours until the day I die."

It was as if I had become invisible, as if I did not exist. As if the proof of all that I offered to my husband, a breathing, squalling mass of infant life, accounted for nothing. Even that wasn't good enough for Hannah.

"I cannot call myself a woman if I never have a child of my own."

She pulled away from him, saying "Let me be," and went off in the direction of the temple. When Elkanah tried to follow, to stop her again, she pushed him away and kept walking. He turned back and saw us all—his wife and children—looking at him, snarled at us. "Go back to your meal," and stomped away to his room.

Hannah stayed away for hours. I rocked the younger ones to sleep, then sat with the older children as they fought then drifted into sleep. By then, the moon hung bright in the sky. When I was a girl, I imagined it was a round-faced, smiling woman. The sky was her black hair, each star a flash of light escaping from behind her as her tresses waved around her head. I had forgotten that vision until I stood from my children's bedside that night in Shiloh. The memory of it—looking up from outside my father's door—filled me with serenity such as I hadn't felt in years. I had never shared that image with anyone. I had never had anyone to share it with.

I went into my room, removed the cloth from my hair and brushed it out so that it lay against my back and

waist. I washed my face, under my breasts and armpits.
I waited for Elkanah to come in, as he always did the
night after offering his sacrifice, but he never came.

Instead, I heard Hannah return. Even from behind my closed door, I sensed a difference in her, an
unfamiliar lightness to her tread. Our husband must
have known it, too. Only a few minutes later, I heard
him go into her room. As I tied my hair back up into
its cloth, I was thankful for the inn's thick stone walls
that kept the sounds of their love from me, at least for
one night.

The trip back home was much as it always was.
Elkanah doted on Hannah. I tended the children. We
three barely spoke to one another. My husband, I could
see, had not forgiven me for upsetting his first wife.

By the time we arrived, I could barely stand from
exhaustion. It was getting harder. Every day, going about
my duties, and every moment holding in everything my
mind thought, my mouth wanted to say. When I caught
sight of myself in the water of the well, I saw an old
woman staring back. She looked haggard and sad. I
hadn't even passed my twenty-fifth year.

That vision of myself stayed before my eyes. For
weeks, I saw it when I rose. I caught sight of that crone
reflected in my children's eyes, though they jumped on
me, hung from my arms, begged me to swing them
around as they always had. Only I saw the change.

All the while, Hannah's skin flushed with color. Her cheeks looked redder, her skin plumper. She laughed as I had never seen before, not saving it for her nights with Elkanah, but out in the open. Soon enough, I saw how her breasts swelled, and I knew, perhaps even before Elkanah. Maybe even before Hannah herself, who had never felt the changes that pregnancy brings to a woman's body.

There was great celebration in the house of Elkanah during the months before Hannah's baby came. He made sure she had cushions on which to sit, monitored her meals to ensure that she ate enough, placed his hand on her growing stomach. His eyes jumped in surprise when he felt movement there for the first time.

My own belly lay flat under my hand for the first time since I had entered his home. He didn't come to my bed any more.

I despaired of the future, of watching husband and wife focus on their darling child, while my children and I were left to sweep up the ashes of Elkanah's affection. During those long months of Hannah's fullness, I lost even my bitterness. Sorrow, I learned, is the stronger emotion. My invisibility had become complete. And since I could not be seen, I stopped attending to myself. I didn't bother washing my hair or clothes. I left my room only to cook and care for my children, then lay back down in my bed until evening, when I gathered them around me again for the night. No one took note of my absence.

What I feared most was the day the midwife arrived to help Hannah with the birth. Her son would become the princeling of the house. Her standing with our husband would be elevated even more than before. I was locked away in my own lonely misery and so I missed the signs of change as they slowly came.

Until Elkanah began coming to my bed again. So many months had passed, and the only touch I had felt was from children. It seemed as if all of a sudden he was ravenous for me. I never heard the whispering and laughing from his room when Hannah went in to him. It took a few more weeks, and then one day I realized that she hadn't been in there since before her son was born.

After that, I began venturing out of my room. I washed my hair, mended the rips in my dress. My entrance back into the family was driven by curiosity. I wanted to see what had happened to drive Elkanah back to me, but this was the first thing that piqued my curiosity in so long that I snatched at it.

Hannah seemed unconcerned. She sat by the fire with her baby, whom she had named Samuel, running her hand over his down-covered head, as taken with his every sneeze, every smile, every shift of his arms or legs as any new mother. Our husband went about his business as he always had, praising the Lord for his good fortune. He didn't approach her or take the child from her arms to cradle him. He didn't bend over Hannah's shoulder to gaze at their precious boy.

Now there were three spheres in our household. Elkanah stood on his own, Hannah and Samuel, and I with my children. The only contact between us came when Elkanah's body entered mine.

I saw him begin to speak to Hannah once or twice, to reach for her hand, but she didn't look up at him. She pulled her hand back to cradle their baby, hummed softly to him, and barely noted her husband's presence by her side. After that, Elkanah didn't approach her any more.

By then, he had planted his seed in me again. I was slowed by the sluggishness of early pregnancy. The bile of acid rose in my throat. Still, Samuel suckled at Hannah's breast.

He grew as I did, laughed for the first time, rolled over, crawled. When the midwife came to me, Hannah's boy had begun to pull himself up onto his feet by grabbing hold of his mother's lap. She laughed and clapped her hands to see him do it.

If I had ever harbored a secret thought that motherhood would change her, that we would sit together, companionable with our babies, I discarded it soon enough. I thought back to my mothers, their eyes streaming with tears as they laughed over some silly thing a child had done, or a joke about my father that only women who shared the same man could understand. I thought back to running to any one of them, whether she had birthed me or not, when I fell and cut my shin, how she pulled me into her lap, washed out the dirt and held me until my crying had stopped. My children would know no such comfort from Hannah.

She would have nothing to do with me. Still. Even in her great joy, she let me know my place in her house. "She will get my boy sick," she said of my latest infant, and carried him away. "Tell your brats to stay away from Samuel," she snapped, after my older children tried to play with her son.

He will grow up very lonely, I thought, if she denies him the companionship of even his brothers and sisters. Nor would she make new ones for him if Elkanah kept away from her bed. He told her to hand the baby to me, but she said no. He demanded that she leave her son, if only for an hour, but she refused. She would not be separated from her child.

Elkanah's smile faltered. He became a new man, uglier and angrier than I had ever seen him. He shouted at the children. His touch became rough at night. Finally, he exploded in rage.

"You have an unnatural attachment to that baby." He thundered at Hannah, who had been absorbed in her

son's antics as always. "You have forgotten your duties
as a wife."

"Aren't you happy now?" she asked. She seemed
truly puzzled, as if she had not even noticed all the tension that had been growing around her. "I have given
you a fine son. Isn't that what you wanted?"

"It is what you wanted! But it has made you forget
who you are. My wife."

"And his mother."

"My wife."

I stood in the doorway behind Elkanah and saw the
whole thing. He was furious, she resentful. I saw as he
rushed to her and grabbed Samuel out of her embrace.
He clutched the boy's arm tight enough to make him
cry out. "Let him go," Hannah said. "You've gone mad."

She ran at him, tried to pry his grip loose, but it
was only when Elkanah lifted the boy as if to fling him
against the wall that I rushed in. I acted on instinct. No
one should hurt a child, no matter what his mother has
done, how she has tortured me. Hannah was too small
to stop Elkanah on her own, but together we pulled the
boy away from him.

Hannah hugged him and rushed to the other end of
the room, Samuel sobbing into her shoulder. I couldn't
believe this man was my husband, who had always been
mild-mannered, who spent his days praising the Lord
for all he had been given. The man in front of me was

possessed of something evil. It drenched his skin in a sheen of oily sweat, distorted the planes of his face. He snarled. Spit flew from his mouth when he spoke.

He pointed to me. "She understands. Even with all her children, she gives me my due." But I would not be a bludgeon to be used between them anymore, and he no longer deserved my attention. I turned from him and addressed her.

"He will hurt your boy eventually if you don't do something," I said. For the first time since I came into Elkanah's home, she answered me without adding an insult.

"What can I do? He is my son. I waited so many years for God to answer my pleas."

Neither of us had the answer. Elkanah's displeasure with Hannah had not increased his affection for me, but at least I could distract him. Every night, I went into his room whether he called me or not. He was not young when I came into his household, and age had overtaken him in the years since then. I gave my body to him so often at night that he was too tired to feel anything for his first wife or her son during the day.

The sun rose and set, rose and set, until the time came for us to go to Shiloh again. Despite Elkanah's newfound impatience, we went up as usual. He chose the finest ewe, led her by a rope himself as we made the trip.

At the temple, the priests greeted us, praised Elkanah on the great bounty that God had given him.
"So many fine children," the high priest said, as if he
had something to do with their coming into the world.
When his eyes alighted on Hannah, his satisfaction
seemed to grow even greater.

"So this is the young man you prayed for," he said,
and took the boy from her arms, held him up in the air
to make him giggle, and then returned him to Hannah.
"He is a fine boy who will bring merit to his parents'
names and to his people. You have much to be thankful
for this year."

Elkanah sucked in his breath. Hannah's face twisted
at the cruel irony of the priest's words, but they gave me
the solution to our problems, a way to protect the boy.

"Leave him here," I said to her after the evening
meal.

Her brow furrowed. It took her a moment to understand what I was talking about. "My boy?" she said,
and looked over to where he slept. Desperation and
love seemed to seize her by the shoulders. "I can't. God
finally answered me. Maybe it would be nothing to you
to give up one of your children, but he is all I have. A
mother can't abandon her child."

I had grown calloused to her insults, so it was easy
to ignore this one. "If you love him, you will leave him
here with the priests. Dedicate him to God. The priest

said the boy is destined for great things. They can raise him to that fate better than we can in our small home."

It didn't matter that I enlarged upon what the priest had really said, that I had blown his words up more than he probably intended. Hannah would believe anything about her son.

Hannah hesitated, but she didn't turn away. She listened, so I kept talking.

"The priests will care for him. God will watch over him. He is not safe in our home. Soon, even you won't be safe."

When I made her the object of discussion, her eyes flared with some of their old anger. "You just want him out of the way so that your children will be the only ones Elkanah cares for."

I sighed. I had suffered so much at the hands of this woman, and still she abhorred me, but I was no longer the hated second wife. We were equal now, if only because our husband held back his affection from both of us.

"I have no love for you," I said. After all these years, she still couldn't see the truth of our lives, "but I am trying to help you."

There was no more for me to say, and I had to be back in my room. Elkanah would expect me to be waiting for him. Being in the presence of the priests and bringing the sacrifice seemed to have returned him to a semblance of himself. He remembered his piety, and with it his mood lightened. His caresses were gentler that night than they had been in months. I was almost deceived into believing there was some emotion in them, but I had learned enough by then to know better.

The next morning, I was in a frenzy of work packing our family up to return home. When all the donkeys were loaded with their burdens, all the children accounted for, and the innkeeper assured that we had left his rooms in good condition, we began the long walk home. I didn't notice Hannah until we were on the road. She sat on her donkey as if her body weighed too much for her. Her arms hung limply at her sides. They swung back and forth to the rhythm of the ass's footfalls as if they were not attached to her shoulders. She looked ahead, but it was as if her eyes saw nothing.

It was then I saw that her son was not strapped to her back. I looked again. Her arms were empty, too. She had listened to what I said. I marveled at it, but she didn't acknowledge me. I knew then that I would never learn what had changed her mind. As bad as things had been between us before, they were bound to get worse. She had sacrificed the best of herself, had lost her boy even if it was to save him. Even though I had been the one to save him, she would blame me for his absence for the rest of our lives.

Elkanah must have seen what she had given up for

him, or known of her intentions before we set out. As always, they kept their confidences from me. He rode over to her, took her hand in his and ran his fingers over the skin of her forearm. He pulled in close to her, whispered into her ear as he used to do. She didn't respond, but she allowed him to hold onto her, to adore her as he always had.

Everything, I saw, was returning to how it had been. To normal. The road stretched out before us. We had two long days of walking ahead of us. I tightened the cloth that held my baby to me, felt the warm heft of her against my shoulder, and labored on.

# SAUL'S DAUGHTER

*"Her husband walked with her as far as Bahurim,*
*weeping as he followed her;*
*then Abner ordered him to turn back,*
*and he went back."*
2 Samuel 3:16

———◆———

**Gallim**

Life happens slowly in a small village. Our bonds of family and clan run deep. We take care of each other here. The content of each person's heart seems open for all to read. We live and we die here. The men bring their brides to dwell among us. We care for the widow, feed her at our tables when there is no one left to provide for her. We give the orphan a place to sleep, find him a wife, become the parents he needs us to be.

Our village, Gallim, is a quiet place. We are used to the slow rhythms of our corner of God's world, to the vistas of terraced fields, pasture, and mountains unbroken by a city wall. It was like all the other villages that dotted the Judean hills, tiny outposts whose young men were often away fighting our unseen enemies, Philistine to the west, Moab to the east, who could scale the hills and overrun us if we didn't stay vigilant. Nonetheless, the struggles of the kingdom rarely entered.

Hills remain sturdy. They never move, though we scamper over their surfaces. To them, there is no difference between us and our animals. The goats jump higher, sheep bend to the grass, and we tread heavily. What is that to the soil, which will renew itself long after we are gone?

————◆————

### Palti

It took time for me to convince Michel that my love was sincere. "You are here now," I said. "You are my wife, part of my home, my family."

"You are kind," she replied. "I have not deserved the welcome your family has given to me. I will forever be grateful to you, and to them."

It was not what I wanted to hear. Gratitude is what
a man feels for his savior. It is the emotion of strangers
unless accompanied by something deeper—affection,
shared purpose, love.

"Please," I begged, "you are mine, and I am yours.
Nothing will change that."

Her reticence was not hard to understand, and I felt
for her. Life had not been kind to her. I am a patient
man, but even I have my pride. It took considerable
persistence to let her come to me. It was like coaxing a
wild animal—platefuls of food left out, and each night
the bowl a little closer, until finally, it is inside and no
longer afraid. That's only half-right. She was aloof, but
not skittish. Warm to everyone, including me, but she
held a piece of herself back, would not allow herself to
be comfortable in my company. She was sure, I saw,
that I would prove myself like the other men she had
known, who made use of her and then, when she was
no longer valuable, walked away.

I had watched her for years. When I was still young
and of sound body, I served our king as all other young
men do. I was fast and fearless. I was also loyal, a trait I
have carried with me all my life. When I entered Saul's
service, I signed my existence over to him. He was a wise
leader, a forceful man who had united the restive tribes
under one rule. We were stronger when we fought as one
than we had been as scattered clans, each vying for its

own glory. I admired him for seeing that, for being able
to act on it.

Soon after my induction, I was noticed by Saul's
highest general, Abner. He watched me throw a spear
and wrestle others to the ground. He saw that I stayed
calm in the confusion of a fight and that I was not loud
and intemperate, but kept my own counsel. Which is
how I came to be part of the king's own detail. We
served longer than others, stayed in the capital while
the young men around us went home to marry and raise
families. We took oaths to hold his life dearer than our
own, to march into battle with him, to protect him.

It was the first time I had lived in a city. Not just
any city. The capital itself, with its winding alleys and
buildings set one atop the next. We were given a place
to sleep inside the walls of the palace, and marched out
every day to practice our maneuvers in the shadow of
the city walls. We followed the king when he left, and
came back with him when he returned. In the evenings,
we filled the dining hall, its thick walls grimed with the
smell of sweaty men that I doubted would ever fade.

That's where I first saw her. She came in with the
other royal women—wives, daughters, and daughters-
in-law—carrying jugs of wine and trays heavy with
food. They wove between us, doing their duty as we did
ours, each as out of reach as the stars in heaven. None
of us dared speak to them. To look at them openly was

to court the king's displeasure. They were his women. We pretended, to the best of our ability, that they were spirits moving among us, magic winds that bore food and drink and then rushed back out, ruffling our hair as they passed.

Of course, we all looked anyway. Asking a roomful of boys not to notice the girls among them is like asking a tree not to grow or the rain not to fall. The trick was not to be caught. So we perfected the art of ducking our heads and looking out from beneath our hair, catching sight of what parts of them we could. Slender ankles and sandal-clad feet. The hems of dresses that swung around shapely calves. Brown arms as they lowered plates in front of us. And, in the quickest of glances, faces, necks, hair. They were as beautiful as they were untouchable. They made us moan with desire.

I didn't take any notice of Michel at first. She was still just a girl, nine or ten years old, with brown hair that swung against the middle of her back, and dark, serious eyes. If I looked at any of them, it was at her older sister, just as everyone else did. Merav was a great beauty, one of those girls who understood the power of her position as eldest daughter of the king from her earliest years. She was also bound by her father's expectations to stay away from his men, and yet she managed to gather all the boys' attention to her, to spread it behind her as she passed like a perfume she wasn't yet old enough to wear.

Michel didn't draw attention to herself. She carried cups and wine as duty demanded, but she had been overshadowed by her older sister and her brother, the crown prince, from the moment of her birth. Jonathan already sat next to the king each night, a young warrior in love with his own expanding possibilities. From where I sat among the men, it was clear how much easier it was to be heir to the throne than to be king. Saul was rarely anything other than sober, even in the rowdy company of his men, but Jonathan jumped into the camaraderie of army life from the first. About my age, he was like his father, taller and more handsome than the rest of us combined, but he had a loud, quick laugh and slapped the other boys on the back whether he knew our names or not.

Some of my brothers-in-arms took nothing but pride in what we did. They competed among themselves to see who could fight harder, feel less. I couldn't help but notice that the vows I had made—to swear off marriage and the comforts of a woman's embrace—so that I would be prepared to fight, to die if that's what it came to, were made in order to protect my king's right to surround himself with all these women. It's what a soldier does. He doesn't question. He does what he is told, then takes his wages and helps care for his family.

The king's women made a great show of ignoring us, but the capital was full of non-royal girls who were happy to toss their hair for our benefit and smile at us as we passed through the city gates. As warriors, we walked as if we, and not the man we served, owned everything within our reach.

Within a few years, Michel had changed. Where Merav stayed small and lush in imitation of her mother, Michel shot up. Her shoulders broadened, her lips became—or so it seemed to me—more full. Most of the men still panted after her sister. They made up secret names for her so they could discuss her openly without anyone knowing. She became the topic of extended conversation, and no one the wiser that they spoke so freely about the king's daughter.

I didn't need any nicknames for Michel. The men around me would look at any young woman when she passed, including Michel, but she seemed not to notice. It became hard to tell if she didn't feel our eyes on her, or if she accepted our attention as what was naturally due to her. Looking around at these boys and men with whom I shared every moment of my life, I felt as if I was the only one who studied her, my eyes drawn to her as if of their own volition. I'm not sure she knew I existed. I lived with a constant fear that she would catch me staring, and held my head even lower. It wouldn't surprise me if she wouldn't even be able to recognize my face. I never gave her the chance to get a good look at it.

I had been away from the capital for some time when

I learned of her marriage. Of course, even in our small village, we had heard about David, the boy who came out of nowhere to become the nation's great hero, its latest savior. I'd seen him, too, on my trips to the capital with our family's wool and sheep. My father had always had a place of honor among the merchants at the back of the dining hall. Once he died, I took his seat. From there, I saw David. Short, slim, and burnished from a life in the sun, he walked with the assurance of a man twice his size. People wanted to be near him. When I served in the army, the greatest assignment had been to Saul's own troop. Now, the men fought to be chosen for David's.

Even the royal women, as bound by the king's decrees as every man in that room, couldn't hide the attention they paid to him. I had studied Michel with the intensity of a holy text for long enough to see how she noticed him too, and how she tried to hide it, just as I had done for so long when looking at her.

He accepted the adulation as if he was born to it. Only a few years younger than I am, and so unschooled in the way of war, and yet, each time I visited, he was more comfortable in the capital and the army.

Even after I was forced to leave the king's service, I still knew many of the warriors who served him and talked with them in the hours after the evening meal. Those who had been assigned to David's regiment

crowed about their prowess. The ones who marched
with Saul or Abner grumbled about David. "His rise in
the ranks has been suspiciously quick," they complained
to me. "I worked for years, and here he's mastered a
sword in just months." To top it all off, he played the
lyre and sang. "It's as if," they said, "a girl's fantasy has
come to life to walk among us. He turns us invisible, not
just within the palace, but in the whole city." Girls still
crowded the city gates to greet the soldiers, but they only
wanted to catch sight of David, to dance and sing and
make him take note of them.

When I heard that Saul had given Michel to David
in marriage, my heart sank. I never really thought she
would be mine, no matter what I had done in Saul's
army. No matter my heroics, the loyalty I had paid so
dearly for, I never rose beyond the rank of foot soldier.
I was even relieved to return to Gallim when I did. I
could take care of my mother, my brother, and sisters. I
could hide there, too, so the world didn't need to know
how much less of a man I was than when I had set out
so many years before.

But Michel had been lodged in my mind for so long
it was hard to let her image go, the tall, quiet specter
that drifted through the dining hall and my dreams. It
wasn't right to think about another man's wife, even if
she was so far from my unremarkable life, and even if
no one would ever know where my thoughts wandered

during those long afternoons in the hills.

And so I put her out of my mind, focused on mastering my father's trade, found good husbands for my sisters, and continued to make the trip through the mountains to the capital every season to buy and sell. Each time I went, the soldiers seemed to grow younger, the king older. Where once I was like them, now my clothes and skin never shed the smell of livestock. And there was David, going from one success to another, his days of shepherding flocks, the wind his only companion, long gone. It was impossible not to see how we had traded places. David, the warrior—more famous and beloved than I could ever hope to be—surrounded by adoring underlings. Me, just a rustic goatherd and sheepshearer growing more and more reserved with people as time wore on. I had grown used to the company of my animals, who never had much to say.

But there was a kinship between the two of us, even if only I realized it. I recognized the shepherd he used to be. The quiet assurance that made others want to fill his silences with chatter was familiar to me. Even in those early years, it was clear he was a born leader, the kind of man who knows how to hold his confidences, allow others to foist their ideas and beliefs onto him just enough to make each think that he, not David, had thought up all those notions and plans.

It was an interesting vantage, the back of the dining

room that used to be so familiar to me. Once I had sat at the king's own table every night. Now I saw David's advance only when I came to the capital, my mind focused on the business of pleasing my customers, particularly the king, who made a point of repaying the sacrifice I had made by buying what I had to sell. It was impossible to miss how David seemed to grow in the months of my absence, but no one present at the beginning would have imagined how high he had set his sights. Looking back, the signs were all there from the start. Only Saul saw it, and no one believed him, not even his children.

What could not escape my notice was how changed Saul was, his hair still thick but graying, the skin of his face tightening over his broad cheekbones. There was a wariness in his eyes that was new, too. I didn't pay as much attention as I should have. I may have cast her from my mind, but it was Michel who still held my attention when she passed through the room. Marriage suited her. She had never been like Merav, who wore her marriage to one of Saul's top generals like a crown of victory. Michel just seemed deeply satisfied, as if she had found the answer to a question that had been plaguing her. She seemed even more out of reach than ever, having crossed into a life I thought was closed to me forever.

Not a year later, when I returned to the capital, everything had changed. As usual, I brought a caravan of donkeys weighed down with jugs of oil pressed from our olive groves, pelts and bags of wool, and the best sheep my herds had produced. The market under the walls was as busy as ever. Coins passed into and out of my hand as they always did, but the city was different. Women and girls who had sung and run through the narrow alleys in the past, walked slowly and spoke in hushed tones. When I took my place for dinner, I noticed how stale and motionless the air seemed to have become.

Except for right around Saul, which crackled with his anger. Abner, still at his side, whispered in his ear every few minutes, trying, I could see, to calm him, to soothe his temper. The men in the dining hall, from the oldest and most distinguished to the freshest recruits who still felt the excitement of being in the presence of the king and all the powerful men of Israel, sat like stone altars, barely daring to move. Jonathan, always full of loud joviality, seemed sullen and distracted, his handsome face uncharacteristically anxious. David was nowhere to be seen.

When the women brought the food, I noticed that Michel was absent, too. I couldn't inquire about her, of course, but I trusted everything would become clear eventually. People like to talk in the capital. If you are a man willing to listen, you will hear everything before long. It would have to wait until after what proved to be a silent, tense meal. Until Saul's rage boiled over and he rose as quickly as a man half his age and snatched a spear out of the grip of one of his guards. Abner grabbed at Saul's hand, but it was too late. The king had already flung it at Jonathan, missing his head by inches and lodging it in the wall behind the startled young man.

Jonathan jumped up. His eyes jerked in his head, words desperate to escape his mouth. He swallowed them quickly. A crown prince knows better than anyone when to hold his tongue around the king.

Saul didn't exercise such restraint. "You idiot," he said. "Would you choose him over me? He will take everything from you!"

"He won't, Father," Jonathan said in as calm a voice as a man with a spear stuck in the wall behind him can muster. "We all love and revere only you."

The room cleared quickly, everyone concerned and embarrassed at having seen the king's loss of control. As we filed out, I caught sight of Saul sitting as if depleted in his chair. Abner and Jonathan loomed above him.

Outside, the men exploded with talk. "David is gone," one of my long-known contacts told me. "Saul tried to kill him." Another added, "He threw a spear at David just as he did tonight. What's more, Jonathan and Michel are suspected of treason for helping him escape."

Something had shifted in the months since I had

last passed this way. Saul had always had one eye trained on the many men who would try to usurp his throne. The kingdom was full of ambitious men who would name themselves leader. He had swatted each away in turn. This time, he felt a threat rising within his own home. Saul had dropped any pretense of love for David. He regarded David as a threat, a danger to everyone, most of all to himself.

"Michel hasn't been seen outside the women's house in weeks." The men around me had so much information. They detailed the political maneuvering of the kingdom in minute detail, but not one of them could tell me what had become of her beyond that bare fact.

Only I would learn the truth. That very night, Saul summoned me to his room. I didn't even know he was aware of my presence in the capital. I had only seen him once since I'd arrived, and that was at dinner a few hours earlier when he had been distracted by dramas in which I was not a player. I should have known better. Never underestimate the king. I had lived by that mantra while a soldier. Civilian life had caused me to forget.

At first, I thought he was alone, but the room was dark. A single torch lit the entire space. As the shadows settled themselves, I could distinguish the outlines of a chair, armor propped up against the back wall. Even in the half-light, I could make out the braid of my wool woven into the wall hangings. The silhouette of a person, crouched as if ready to bolt, revealed itself against the walls. My heart leapt and shrank at once. I had never been this close to Michel before.

"Thank you for coming," Saul said when I had entered. He seemed relaxed, in command of himself, once more the king I had known and served.

"I'm honored to be in your presence, my Lord," I answered, not knowing what he could possibly want from me, why I was in a room with only him and his daughter.

"You are a good man, Palti. I can think of no one I would rather call 'son' than you. Leave all your goods with me. I will buy everything you have brought to the capital. Marry my daughter," he pointed to Michel. "Take her home with you."

Saul's behavior in the dining hall earlier that evening had been shocking, out of character, but even that could not have prepared me for what he had just asked of me. Rumors that the king had become increasingly eccentric had been murmured throughout the kingdom for years. This, I saw, was proof of something much deeper.

"Your Majesty," I said, stumbling over my words. "I am diminished." I began again, "I am not fit for marriage. And your daughter," I continued, unable to even say the words as they formed. I didn't see a spear nearby, but Saul was still a large, strong man who could easily hurt me if I said the wrong thing. If his sudden anger at his own son was any indication, almost anything could set him off. He knew what I was going to say, though. He must have known that any man he brought into this room would think the same, but he brushed off my concerns. "Think nothing of the past," he said. "Even a widow may remarry. Her former husband is dead to us all. You will marry her and take her back to your village."

My head reeled. Had there been more light in the room, it probably would have caused my vision to blur. All my youthful fantasies were being offered to me as if on a platter. I wondered if I had not hidden my regard of Michel as well as I had thought, if the king had noticed it and allowed it for reasons known only to him. At the same time, I knew what this meant—I was to be the means of Michel's banishment. And yet, what choice did I have? He was my king. I had followed him into battle. I still believed in him.

The king called Michel forward into the dim light that the torch threw over us. She unfolded herself from the floor, stood as tall and straight as I had ever seen her, and came to my side. She was not the woman I had longed for years ago. Her hair hung lifeless against her face. Her eyes were red and swollen, the skin on her cheeks and forehead blotchy over a pale base. When Saul gestured to me, I wrapped my mantle around both our shoulders, drawing her closer to me than any woman had ever stood. She smelled of salt and cinnamon. The king told me to take her hand in mine. I grasped my useless right wrist in my left hand, lifted it, and placed my fingers into her waiting palm.

———————◆———————

## Gallim

We watched her with interest, this city girl dropped into our quiet country life. Gallim is a small village, just a handful of stone and mud houses on the side of a mountain. It is too small even to have a wall around it. Even the old ones can't remember a time when we didn't need a lookout at the highest spot to watch out for encroaching enemies.

We couldn't imagine what it must be like to go from a life at the crossroads of world, where people stream in and out as they make their way north to south, east to west, to the handful of windworn faces she encountered here. The inhabitants of the capital alone numbered more than most of us lived with for the entirety of our lives. Poor girl, we thought, to go from a city, surrounded by a thousand people, to this outpost.

Any young woman brought up in a bustling metropolis would find us backward. How much more so, then, the daughter of the king? At first, she tried to hide her identity from us, but there was always something different about her, even if she tried to tamp it down, to erase it. A person's beginnings always leave their mark. Nothing is hidden in a small town. Secrets are hard to keep.

Palti had sent word that he would be bringing a bride home with him, but he said nothing about her. We rejoiced, of course, all of us. He was our greatest son, a hero to king and country. He had taken his father's place in his home and on the council of town elders with grace, but he came back from war so different than the strapping young man he used to be. His mother despaired that no family would allow its daughter to marry him, though we all knew him to be kind, responsible, and let's not forget, rich in land, animals, and gold. He had grown too quiet, had absorbed himself in his work. He let the village boys clamber up his torso and hang on his left arm like a tree. He trained the young men, was sober and serious when deliberating the town's affairs. But he carried a bubble of solitude with him everywhere. No one had been able to pierce it.

He was the best that Israel had to offer, and yet, a moment's action determined his fate. We watched him struggle to accept his new body, the life it held out for him. We saw his anger, then his deflated resignation. We thought he had given up on himself and that others would follow his lead, until the day we learned he had married. We prepared a feast, gave a shout when we saw them wind up the goat paths in the distance, Palti at the head of his train of donkeys, a servant at the back, and riding on the foremost ass, a woman, her head cloaked against the wind.

We only got a good look at her when they were in the center of town. All activity stopped. We were too curious to pretend this was an event like any other. It was strange, we thought, how she kept her head down, her hands tucked firmly into her sleeves. Perhaps, we thought, she was shy, as a new bride brought to her husband's home often is, but her posture, rigid as a cedar, told another story.

"This is my wife, Michel," Palti told us, after he had led the girl to his mother, who sat with the other women around the last of the oven's fire. They had been baking a last loaf of bread, stirring a final pot of lentils. His mother, beaming, took the girl's hands into her own. She tried to pull them back, or to turn them so that only the backs would show, but her palms peeked upward just long enough for some of us to catch sight of the darkened skin, tinged blue and shading into purple in their creases.

That set us all talking. Long after everyone had eaten and sung marriage songs in honor of the new couple. Long after everyone had filed by them, each greeted with a smile by Michel, our newest villager, who sat in state as if she had been here all along and we were the awkward newcomers, we retired to our houses and noted with raised eyebrows the curious fact of her dyed skin, glimpsed ever so briefly, but not to be denied.

Over the next few days, Michel joined the women each morning to stoke the fire, gather the water, and bake the bread. She kept her hands hidden away, and even when the other women removed their sandals to wash their tired feet before the evening meal, she kept hers on, offered to pour the water over everyone else's dusty ankles, then politely declined when we offered to reciprocate.

She was a mystery to us. Friendly to everyone, from the oldest woman who wandered aimlessly around the houses, entering each as if it were her own, to the babies still wrapped in swaddling. She sat with the youngest mother, who had also been brought to our town as a wife recently, and cooed over the infant's chubby hand, his toothless smiles, but she gave no clue about her life before the day she entered our circumscribed world. She had no stories to tell, never let slip a small detail from girlhood about her parents or some passing moment that had never left her. It was as if, we marveled, she came to us without a past.

We were equally curious about her new marriage. It was obvious that she and Palti did not know one another well when he brought her to live with us, but many brides are strangers to their husbands on the day of their marriage. Michel was as polite with him as with us all. It was Palti who surprised us. Normally the most reserved of men, he courted her openly, bringing dogwood blossoms to her at the end of the day, a newborn lamb to live as their pet. She laughed at the animal's antics, and swept it into her arms. Still, we couldn't shake the sense that she was ready to leave at a moment's notice. That she didn't think her time with us would last.

Time passed, and she remained. Eventually, she relaxed, as people will do. There was still a faraway sense to her, which we attributed to homesickness for the excitement of her city youth. And then came the day, inevitable perhaps, when she didn't hide her palms from us, and she removed her sandals to rinse her feet. The color had faded, but it was still there. Finally, we saw what we had all suspected since that first night. Michel wasn't just a city girl married off to a wealthy sheepherder. This girl was royalty. We were sheltered here on the side of our mountain, but even we knew enough of the kingdom to know that only the wives, sisters, and daughters of the king were allowed to touch the dye used for his clothes and the grapes crushed for his wine. Before Michel came to live with us, those women were like mythical creatures to us. They filled the stories the old ones told us late at night, beautiful girls who knew nothing of labor except for the warmth of linen on their fingers and cold grapes beneath their feet. Now we knew that they were real. One walked among us.

Eventually, the whole truth came out. Not just a relative of the king, but his daughter, who had been married to David, the man we had once adored. We looked to Palti as if he were a new man, too, someone we never knew before. He never spoke of a bride price, even though that was the kind of gossip that usually passed freely around a small community. Nor did he say how he came to have her as his wife.

———————◆———————

### Palti

I was prepared to love Michel from the start. I had been ready since those days of surreptitious staring in the dense air of the king's dining hall. We had our first conversation on the day-long walk back to Gallim. I had tied the donkeys together and set my servant at the back to keep them in line. They were obstinate beasts who would stop to rest in a patch of shade or grab at a tuft of grass, but always out of sync with each other. While seven walked, one would refuse to move. When we finally got him going, another would twitch her ears, snort loudly, and plant her feet. As always, their saddle-bags were filled with pots and spices, all the things we didn't produce in Gallim. My return would be different than it had ever been. I could only imagine the celebration the village women would have waiting for us, but I couldn't ignore the original purpose of my trip. My people depended on me to bring these supplies. Each season, the women took stock of what we had, and then parceled it out to make it all last until my next foray to the capital.

I was more anxious to return this time than usual, both to take Michel away from the capital as quickly as possible and to bring her into her new home, so we prodded the asses when they became obstreperous and kept up a steady pace. Michel walked for most of the day. I walked on one side of the lead animal, the sturdiest and most reliable of the bunch. She walked on the other, her hand resting against the donkey's flank.

"My father has spoken of you," she said.

I was surprised. I had always thought myself almost invisible, just one of the many young men who cycle through the capital and the king's home.

"He said you are reliable, that you've proven yourself a good Israelite." Then she laughed, a sound I would come to know well, a deep hum from the back of her throat that indicated less mirth than knowing mockery. "Although what kind of a reward he imagined it must be to give over his disgraced daughter to you, I can't imagine."

"Do you think he hates you?" I had to know. This was more insight into the king's heart than I had ever been given.

"Not him," she said, waving the question away as irrelevant. "He has never given a moment's thought about me beyond my usefulness to him. It's the people who hate me. They wouldn't stand to see me in the city any longer, and so he found a way to send me away."

"Surely, your father feels affection for you," I said. Fathers love their children. This was a fact I knew as surely as the color of the sky or the sheep's birthing season.

She gave that laugh again, looked at me over the ass's back. It was the first time she and I had ever looked directly at one another. "When I was a child, my mother told me that I was not like other little girls, that the regular rules don't apply to daughters of the king. I thought she meant we were privileged, that we were meant for greater things. Now I realize how kind she was being, but she hid the truth from me. There's not a girl alive who really has freedom over her own life. They are bartered away for a sheep or a plot of arable land. But Saul's daughters are hemmed in like no others. We are at the mercy of history and the men who would trade us like prizes."

It was hard for me to listen to her, struck as I was by the directness of her gaze, the way her eyes glistened, black as brined olives, but I paid close attention. She was so young to have this much bitterness eating at her soul, I thought, but I couldn't say anything in return. Her life to that point had given her reason to think that way. So I stayed silent.

"There is a strict hierarchy," she continued. "My sister was the real trophy. To be given her as a wife meant something. I have always been a second-best reward. Merav and I once thought our lives would unfold in a series of golden-hued dreams. Both married to great warriors, our lives dedicated to the future of Israel. As always, she got the dream, and I learned how silly girlish plans can be. Aren't you glad," she said, turning to me again, a crooked smile on her lips, "to know how highly your king esteems you now?"

Perhaps she was right. But Saul had married her to David first, whose reputation was only growing at the time. Even in Gallim, the girls and women sang songs about his exploits. I began to ask about him, to question her logic, but my lips closed on the words. I didn't want to begin this marriage by learning how much more she still loved someone else.

We continued to walk. The hills grew steeper. We passed rows of tall scrub oaks and wended our way through Gallim's olive groves. Eventually, I insisted that she mount the donkey's back, which is how we rose past the terraces and entered the village, Michel astride the animal. I held the reins and led her into town.

When we entered Gallim, I saw it as if through her eyes. It was just a tiny speck of a village. Immediately, she was the focus of everyone's attention. I watched her gather herself, and thought, this is what bravery looks like. She greeted each friend and relative of mine, ate the food that they had prepared for our arrival, cheered the boys and girls who sang for our delight, but I could see how it wore on her. In a single day, the life that she knew, the one she had expected, had been snatched from her.

Finally, I announced that we were tired. "It's been a long day. Go home, friends. Tonight's celebration doesn't mean we won't have to wake up for work early tomorrow morning."

I led her past the smaller houses to my home. It sat at the top of the village, the largest structure in Gallim. I showed her around, the fire pit and cistern outside, pointed out the room my mother and younger brother shared, and then took her into the room I had slept in alone for so many years.

"You can take this room," I said. "I'll sleep elsewhere until you're comfortable in my home." I hoped she liked it in there. Thick woolen hangings in ochre and brown covered the walls to keep the cold out. The heavy blanket on the bed was woven from the softest wool our sheep produce. My mother had left a jug of wine and some bread on the floor for her, in case she woke up hungry in this strange place.

"That's a nice gesture," she said. "But I'm just another Israelite wife now. I'm not the first to be brought far from home to lie in her husband's bed."

That wasn't the answer I had expected. She lay down on the bed. It seemed to me to be a gesture of resignation rather than eagerness.

I am a man of few words. It has never been easy for me to speak about myself. The walls of my house are made of thick limestone. No one could hear us, but I found myself whispering. Michel couldn't understand what a gift she was offering to me. "I am damaged," I said. "I thought I'd never marry."

She had to have noticed my dead arm right away, but so far, she had pretended not to see how it hung limp by my side, stripped of muscle, and useless. I didn't give her a chance to ask about it now. "The priests would reject any sacrifice I brought. I thought I would die childless."

She sat up in alarm. "I will be your wife," she said. "I will stand by your side and lie in your bed. But I can never have your children."

"I don't understand," I said. Confusion wiped away all my other thoughts. Would everything I thought about the world be turned over by this woman? "That's for God to decide."

When she answered, her voice was firm, unyielding. I had heard that tone many times. It was the way Saul spoke when he made a pronouncement that was sure to elicit complaints. "Women and God have always worked together in bringing life into this world," she said.

"But why?" I had finally been given a chance to have a life like other men. It was being taken from me before it even began.

There was cruelty in her voice when she replied. "No matter where I am or who you are, I will always be Saul's daughter. Any children of mine will be caught up in that lineage, no matter who their father is."

"You are my wife now," I said, as if that alone could push away any other reality. "I don't have much to offer, but I will give you the fullest life I can."

I barely knew her. I had only the smallest glimpse into what she had suffered, but I wanted to show her that I wasn't like the other men she had known, that she could trust me.

She must have seen what a blow her words had struck in me. "I'm sorry," she said. I saw that she meant it, although it didn't sting any less. "It's the only way."

—————◆—————

## Gallim

We watched them become closer and finally understood the strength of their bond, but even after we knew the truth, they never discussed her past with us. No one can know what happens behind the closed door of a marriage, not even in a place as small as Gallim. Some secrets can still be kept, and they guarded hers until the very end.

We never spoke of it, never convened a meeting to hash out differences or develop a plan. We were of one mind. Boys continued to go up to the watchtower to scan the hills for encroaching enemies, burdened with the responsibility of our increased danger. As always, there were Philistines, Ammonites, and Moabites who would come to snatch our lands. Now we had to protect her, as well. For a long time, we didn't know what we were protecting her from, but we are fierce in our fidelity here. From the moment she walked into this collection of buildings that we call home, she was ours. We would never give her up without a fight.

———•———

### Palti

I wanted to resist, to win her heart first, but I was still a young man. I had been denied the pleasures of a woman's body, first as part of my pledge to Saul and then because of my injury. And there she was, lying beside me every night, giving her body to me as she had promised.

I tried to be gentle and to give her pleasure. We were alike, she and I. We both had our losses. We both wore their signs on our hands, mine withered, hers blue. I'm not proud to say that I hoped even sadness could bring us together. But each time I came to her, I thought I was fighting the memory of another, more vigorous man, a better lover.

As usual when it came to her, I was wrong.

It had been months since I brought her home with me. She seemed more comfortable, as if she had grown used to the smaller boundaries of our lives here. But she remained closed to me, polite and distant, as daughters of the king are taught to be, so I took her to the one place that no one who had ever passed through this area could resist. I took her to see the secret pleasures of these mountains, a patch of pines one hilltop away that we locals knew so well. Gallim lay behind us. The short valley released its scent of flowering jasmine.

When we entered the copse, all of life seemed blotted out. Sound receded. The sun filtered weakly through the dense foliage. I had come here since I was a boy. It was a small place, an acre or two at most, but so different than the landscape around it, where the imprint of our presence was everywhere, from the terraced pastures and fields of barley to the village itself.

Here, I was never the eldest son who was expected to learn the ways of his father's business. In these woods,

I could play my childish games with all the other village children. The boys ran through the trees imagining themselves celebrated warriors, defeated armies lying at our feet. Girls imitated their mothers, draped branches to make small houses, cooked loaves of mud bread. Although we mimicked our parents, none of us knew we were practicing for adulthood, even though we had no idea how different a child's notion of war is from the real thing, with its stink of blood and fear, or that a woman's toil will lose its thrill in the grinding dailiness of her chores.

I led her around the trees, deeper into the thicket. Rocks embedded themselves in the covering of pine needles on the ground. As we stepped, thorns reached up to tear at our ankles and hems. At the top of the hill was a small pond, the water dark and clean. All the local children loved this pool. It was our private sanctuary. We snuck away to swim or bathe, thought of it as our own, away from the demands and tired talk of adults.

Michel breathed deeply. She removed her sandals, lifted her dress to her knees, stepped into the cold water, and discovered what everyone else did in that place. I watched her face empty and then fill again with a look I had never seen. It was how she looked, I realized, when she was alone and at ease. It was the effect of the place, the trees, the water, the cool air, and the distant sun, kept at bay but benevolently present.

I sat on a boulder by the side of the pond, let her wander around its muddy bank. I imagined the wet dirt massaging the skin between her toes. I had felt that chilly comfort so many times.

Eventually, she turned back to me. "Ask what you want about him," she said. It was an invitation, not a challenge. In all the time we had been together, David lay between us, a third member of our marriage, invisible but exerting his unseen influence.

I wanted to know what kept her so wary, why she only put on an act of happiness with my people, when the truth was so different. "What happened?"

"David deserted me. My father burst into our room to kill him. Jonathan had rushed in to warn us, so I shoved David out the window, told him to run. When Saul arrived, he took up so much space it was as if I was alone with a giant. He barely noticed me, but I put my hands on his chest, tried to stall him while my husband ran through the night without a thought to my fate. My devotion was rewarded with a broken rib and bruises all along my spine when my father flung me against a wall.

"David never looked back. Jonathan went to see him one more time. They said goodbye. He didn't even send a message to me."

She moved her foot in the water, caused ripples to spread out from her still center.

"I expected him to take other wives. Powerful men do that. They surround themselves with as many women as they like, each to fulfill another pleasure—money, land, politics, lust. Women like me know from the first not to imagine anything else. But he took me first and said he loved me. I was stupid enough to believe him."

Even then, with her standing in front of me, in the safest place I have ever been, I couldn't force the question I was desperate to ask from my mouth. I could only sneak around it, feeling my tentative way.

"Did he sing to you?" I said.

"At first."

"I can't carry a tune."

"I don't want music."

"He's a great fighter. Some say he's the best we've ever known."

"I'm tired of warriors," she said. "I don't want to be loved like that anymore. A warrior wants victory in everything. Even in love."

She studied my face for a moment. "I hate him," she said. "For what he did to me, to our nation, to my father, who was a good king until this madness overcame him." She waded over to where I was sitting, then touched my shoulder, the indentation that divided the healthy flesh from wasted. She ran her fingers from the base of my neck all the way down my arm, my shame. The shallow muscles twitched but didn't jump, my fingers lay as limp as ever against my thigh where I had rested them. I held still as she explored the wastes of my body that had once held such strength. She took my hand in hers, traced the shrunken flesh. It was her turn to ask what she had held back.

"How did this happen?"

"I saved your father's life. In battle. A Philistine ran up behind him, raised his spear to strike, and I threw myself between them. Not even the healers could say how I survived the wound."

Her cheeks flushed red. "Forgive me. I didn't know. I should have asked sooner. My family has treated you with the same mercilessness it shows everyone. You saved his life. And this is how he repays you, by forcing you take on the burden of marrying me. My family has taken advantage of you too many times."

I thought I understood her at last. "He didn't make me marry you."

"I was in that room with you. He didn't give you a choice. A king usually doesn't."

"I would have married you anyway."

She laughed again, but there was affection in it this time. "The only thing my father told me about you before he sent me off as your wife is that you are a good man. Is this the secret? Are you good because you're too foolish to know better?"

"I didn't know the details, but it was no secret that

you had stood up to the king to save your husband."

"Everyone thought I was a traitor for doing so. Only Jonathan would speak to me after that. Even my mother pretended I didn't exist."

"They're the fools then. You showed how you loyal are, and that you make a fine wife. I hope."

Her dark eyes narrowed, their usual seriousness replaced with something else. Wickedness, I thought, or something kinder. "Do you think I'll have to push you out a window sometime also?"

"Depends who's chasing me, I suppose."

That was the moment something shifted between us, some chasm closed. Michel lifted my hand, as tenderly as she would a newborn baby, and kissed its shrunken palm. She held it like that, as if it were still strong and could grip her back, all the way back to Gallim.

———◆———

## Gallim

We are used to our quiet life here. Danger surrounds us, but that is the nature of life, and no different for us than for anyone else. We turn to God for protection against the ravages of man and nature. But there are no prayers to say, no sacrifices to offer when we turn against each other.

Even our little outpost is not cut off from the world.

Word of the deeds of others makes its way in. We
heard that David had run to Moab. He took his family
and a growing camp of followers with him, a mob of
wanderers that he trained into a personal army, then
sold its services to the highest bidder. Everyone in Israel
abhorred him.

The news came quicker after that. David was always the topic of discussion. We stopped singing odes
to him when we realized he had returned, was menacing
the towns and landowners for protection and gold.
Anyone who stood in his way was cut down and then,
like a conquering general, David let loose his men to
take lands, cattle, women. As if to make sure no one
misunderstood, David buried the owners' bodies and
took their wives as his own while the graves were still
being filled.

We had heard, too, about our proud king's decline.
How he raved, eyes wild, becoming suddenly as strong
as a youth and then sagging again into the despair of
old age. Time proved Saul right. David was after the
crown. The civil war that followed was inevitable,
unstoppable. We stayed loyal, of course. Everyone with
a penny to his name did, while the outcast and bitter
flowed to David, who took them all in, told them they
were God's elect.

Michel had been with us so long by then that we,
to our horror, forgot who she was when the whispering

started. The women sucked on their teeth and spit on the ground when David's name was mentioned, said he was no son of Israel. She sat quietly then, as still as the mountain itself. When we would come to our senses, recall that she had more at stake, that her father and brothers had to battle every day to stave off the growing threat that David presented, we shut our mouths in embarrassment, tried to turn the conversation to the state of the olive harvest or to criticize the knots in the youngest girls' pulled wool. It was no use. There was nothing else to speak of. Israel was at war with itself.

We heard more. Of David's many wives, his ravaging of the countryside. Michel sat still when a messenger, his clothes not yet stiffened with blood, ran into town with the news that Saul and Jonathan had died. She ripped the neck of her dress and put ashes on her head, as a good daughter should, but there was no change in her. She still worked beside us, still laughed with the children and walked hand-in-hand with her husband, put her head close to his to speak as all couples do, the murmured and inconsequential words that bound one to another.

Palti, too, was changed. As their love grew, their comfort with one another gave him back some of the youth he had lost. For so long, he had walked among us as a man marked. He hid behind his work, going out with the flocks as often as possible. We tried to show him that we still esteemed him, but only when Michel came, when she began to look to him in the way of women, did his back unbend, his brow clear. She brought him back to himself and to us, and for that we were thankful.

———————•———————

### Palti

I watched as she slowly grew to love life in Gallim, to be among the women who sleep and wake every day in the same place, confident in neighbors who will feed them in sickness, dance with them in celebration, cry with them after the deaths they will inevitably see. Cry over them when it is their turn to die.

She still wasn't one of them, not really. At night, when we were alone, she would confide in me. "I wish I could put on the grace of their simplicity," she said. "They send their boys off to my father's army believing that if their sons die, it is for something more glorious than the king's latest whim or folly. They wouldn't believe me if I told them the truth, that our world is driven by one man's desires and those wily enough to whisper in his ear. The rest of us get used and discarded."

It hurt me to hear her speak this way. I wanted to think our love would erase the outside world. I thought that with enough time, she would become like the women

I had grown up among.

I still wanted a child. I wanted her to be the mother of my children, but each month she would turn me away from our bed, tell me to return the next week.

I begged her to reconsider. "I've seen how you take the babies of Gallim onto your lap. They all lean into your arms. I watch how you soothe their cries," I said. "You would make a good mother."

"I want to say yes." She looked pained. "But I can't, now more than ever. Not with Saul dead and David stalking the country."

Another man would grow resentful. He might even come to hate her, but I had lived too long without love to pull it from her. I had wrapped her in the folds of my love. Nothing could unwind it.

———— ◆ ————

## Gallim

She lived well among us for a few years. The signs of her old life disappeared. The dye faded from her hands. Her heels were round and pink. She was happy. Until we started to hear what David's ambition had wrought. How many dead, how much taken.

Something broke in her the day a woman staggered into Gallim, collapsed as if she'd run from the other end of the country. She lay panting on the ground as we rushed to pour water over her skin and into her mouth. She had lost her sandals somewhere, leaving the soles of her feet torn and cracked. When she recovered enough to speak, she pulled herself to all fours, pushed back onto her haunches, a tattered heap of a woman, and, ignoring us all, looked straight at Michel.

"You knew me once," she said. "I served you and your sister both. Do you recognize me?"

Michel was caught off guard. This woman was a ragged wretch. Her clothes were shreds hanging off a threadbare skeleton, her hair matted with grease and the dust of the road. Leaves and small twigs caught in its tangles. She didn't talk wildly. She didn't raise her voice, but there was something about her that made the women hold their young children close. She had the reek of death on her. It spilled out of her eyes and mouth. No one would touch the spot where she sat on the ground for fear of infection.

"They're all gone," she said, as if they were alone in the courtyard, though we all crowded around. "They are all taken from us." Her mouth stretched wide then, a death's mask grin, but instead of laughter, loud sobs scraped out of her throat and mouth.

"Men came, twenty at least. And my master was away fighting. It was just women and children. No one there knew how to raise a sword. We didn't own a spear between us. They ran us through. I tried to save her. I swear."

"Who?" Michel asked, but we all saw that she already knew the answer. She was asking for confirmation, as if she needed to hear the words to believe them.

"They grabbed her boys, down to the little one, whose legs still shook beneath him when he walked. She was inside with the baby. God save me from ever seeing such things again!" She wailed again. "I told her to run, but the door was open. She saw them butcher her children. She ran out, clutching her infant, but she couldn't save them. One of the men saw her, snatched the baby out of her arms, dashed him against a wall."

Michel had stood impassive at every evil tiding that had been brought to us. This news made her legs go weak. We caught her, held her up between us.

"I tried to make her flee," the woman continued, "but she wouldn't leave her sons, even though they were lifeless corpses. Reason left her at the end, I'm sure of it," she said, as if offering a small kindness amid a roaring chaos. "She told me to kill her, but I couldn't. I tried to take her by the arm, to drag her away, into the fields. I thought we could run here together. She shook me off, rushed toward the soldiers. Your sister threw herself onto a sword and died with her boys. I have been running since to get here, to tell you."

At first, everyone was silent. Then the keening started, low at first, one woman's wail picked up by another, until all the women of Gallim joined in. We were crying for her loss. Only Michel didn't cry. She stared at the woman on the ground, but it was as if she had gone sightless and saw nothing. Then she turned away, walked to her house, and closed the door behind her.

———— ◆ ————

### Palti

I got back from the pasture as fast as I could. The old women tried to pat my arm, the young to comfort me with looks that showed sympathy and something more, a pain that had become personal. But no matter how they loved her, this was not their loss. Michel bore it alone.

I rushed past them all, ran into our room. She lay on our bed in the dark. I couldn't tell if she was asleep, but she spoke as soon as I walked in.

"I'm next. There's no one else left."

"You're safe here." I tried to assure her. "David is only sending his army for the men who could take the throne from him."

She turned, put her hand to my face, which retained the warmth of my run against the chill of her fingers. "I tried to tell you." There was such sadness in her voice. "I will never be anything other than Saul's daughter."

"You are my wife," I said. "David abandoned you to

your fate. He never looked back."

"There are still men in this country who would follow Saul, even if they had to do it through me."

"Please, my love, have faith. David has forgotten
you." I could hear myself begging, whether of her or of
God I still don't know.

She cried then. She buried herself in me and let
loose all the sorrow of a person whose past has been
destroyed. Michel was all that was left of the house of
Saul, which had rejected her. They had given her to me.

—————— ♦ ——————

## Gallim

She changed after that. We watched her grow thinner, her skin grey as sage leaves. She still rose to
work with us in the morning, came out into the fields to
help with the lambing, sat down to eat at dusk, but she
rushed away to vomit up whatever she ate, then reeled
back to us, her eyes rimmed red, lips chapped and
dry. She always looked on the edge of illness. Finally,
she stopped coming out of her house. Day after day, a
neighbor girl went in to look after her, spent long hours
at her side, along with Palti, the silence he had finally
shook off overtaking him again.

The better part of a year passed. We tried to go on,
but the nation remained in turmoil. David was king in

the south, growing stronger by the day, but the north
still rebelled against him. Gallim was caught on the
border between the two. Our watchtowers were never
empty now. Israel's unrest gave the Philistines and
Ammonites, all our old adversaries, an opening to
wreak more havoc, and we were on our own, loyal to a
dead king, a headless state.

The Moabites came closest. First, the birds took to
the sky in the hundreds, released shrill calls of distress
as they surged away. We saw the smoke before the
flames licked the hilltops and tried to swallow heaven.
Our enemy had set the pines on fire to clear a path
directly to our village. The smell wove thickly into our
lungs. Every villager mourned the loss of that place, the
cool shade and the cold pond. We remembered playing
there as children. Couples wrapped their arms around
each other, clung tight to the memory of loving there
out of sight and protected.

So we were ready for the alarm when one of our
scouts ran down the hill, warning that a band of soldiers
was approaching. The men of Gallim gathered at the
mouth of the town, strongest at the front, to defend us
any way they could. Our relief was great, then, when
we saw who walked toward us. Abner, whom Saul had
trusted, led his men among us. We greeted him with a
cheer, thinking he was our savior, the bearer of the first
good news we'd heard in years.

But we had opened our arms to the devil. He hadn't come to give us comfort, but to rip us apart.

"I'm here to speak to Palti," he said, looking around the crowd. Palti stepped out from among the other men, smiling to see his old captain.

"I've come to take her back to her husband," Abner said, his face hardened even to his former soldier.

"I'm her husband."

"A woman can't be married to two men at once. I wouldn't think I'd have to explain that to you," Abner said, his voice filled with scorn. "But the king thanks you for watching over her so well these past years."

We didn't know what to do, what to say. Michel solved that for us. She pushed her way through the crowd, shoving us aside. We had never seen her like this. Her face was soft and haggard, her hair wild. She looked as if she hadn't slept in days, but she blazed with rage. She shook with it. "You too, Uncle?" she demanded. "You would betray my father's memory, turn away from a lifetime's loyalty?"

Abner looked almost apologetic. The mask of cold detachment dropped from his face. "I am still a soldier. The war is over. David is my king now. He has demanded that his wife be returned to him. I will obey him."

She threw herself at him then. Fury gave her vigor, and she attacked him with her whole body. This, we saw, was the woman who had faced down the king. Too late we realized that she had always been filled with anger, that it lay brimming beneath the surface. How well she hid it from us behind her open-mouthed laughter and love for Palti.

They were matched in height, but he had the advantage of weight and strength, and a lifetime of battle. Abner easily caught her hands, held them tight until Palti intervened, gently removed her from the older man's grip, kept her close by his side.

"Please," Palti begged. "Don't do this. I have given so much and have so little." It was the first we had heard him speak of the sacrifice he had made for king and country. He had held it until that moment, when he needed it most.

"I always liked you," Abner replied. "I wouldn't want to hurt you over this. Don't make me take her by force."

We were shocked at how casually Abner spoke. Palti had no answer to his threat. He could do nothing but hold onto his wife. Abner considered for a moment, then made an offer. It was nothing, an insult, but Palti grabbed at it. "We will take her with us, but you can walk with her for a bit, so you can say goodbye."

We watched them leave, Palti and Michel, their hands grasped tightly to the other, surrounded by soldiers. Their feet kicked dust into the air. Soon, that was all that was left of them.

———————◆———————

## *Palti*

I cried the whole way. I begged Abner to reconsider. I told him Michel and I would leave Gallim, leave Israel, that no one would hear from us again. I told him I just wanted my wife.

Michel walked silently beside me the whole time. Whatever will she had shown before was gone. Her hand clutched mine, but otherwise she seemed slack, emptied out. The fight had left her.

Eventually, she spoke. "Stop. You won't change his mind. We'll lose our last moments together."

Tears fell freely down my cheeks. "Why don't you argue?" I was desperate, angry even at her. "Do you want to go back there, to your *real* husband?"

She stayed quiet, mild no matter what I said. "You have taught me how to love and be loved. I will take that with me, because there will be no love where I am going."

We kept walking. The soldiers had given us a little room. They walked ahead of us and behind us, but we were alone.

"My time with you has been my real life. Everything before, everything that is to come, is nothing. You are the husband of my heart, but you need to forget me now."

I sobbed, "I can't."

"You can. Go home. Take another wife. She will be lucky to have you. Cherish what we've done. There is no fighting this anymore. They'll kill everyone in Gallim if I don't go back to him. They'll burn the village to the ground until nothing is left." She was so resigned, so unlike the woman I had brought into my home years before. She was also right. We were powerless against the new king.

"I'm so sorry," she said. "I wish I had trusted you sooner. I wish you hadn't been drawn into the mess of my life. You have so much left to do." Her voice became urgent. "You must do it. You must do it, because I will never be allowed to again. Do you understand?"

There was so much more I wanted to say, but I did understand. I was crying too hard by then to answer. I nodded. I would obey.

We walked a long way, but we came to the end too quickly. I could see David's camp on the next ridge. It spread over the entire mountain, a dragon with a fearsome head and a mighty tail.

"This is as far as you go, Palti," Abner said. There was no malice left in him. It seemed he even felt bad for me. "Don't make this harder on yourself than it has to be. Go home, man. Don't make so much fuss over a woman."

There was no answer I could give him. There was nothing I could say to a man who didn't understand why I would want this woman, how she had freed me from myself, had opened me to life after I had given up on it. He pulled her hand from mine. I stood frozen as they made their way into the valley, my last sight of her clouded by my own tears.

———◆———

## Gallim

We mourned her loss. We tore our clothes, draped ourselves in ashes. We knew she was as lost to us as if she had died. We tried to console ourselves with memories of her beauty, her resilience. The elders pointed to the smoldering patch where the pines used to stand, reminded us that it was David's forces that had pushed the Moabites back and kept them from destroying us. "Be thankful," they scolded. "He could have been angry, but he chose mercy."

We pretended loyalty after that, sent our boys to fight in his army, our taxes to fill his treasury. When guests came through Gallim, we sang songs of praise to Israel's king. But during the long seasons of windy isolation, we remembered Michel, and how we had sheltered her. She had walked among us like a queen, left us like a ghost. It's hard to keep a secret in a village, but we keep hers yet.

Palti is still the best among us. He married the neighbor girl, who is sweet and yielding. She brought him out of his grief. They are raising three girls. The oldest walks shoulder to shoulder with him now, her brown hair tapping against the middle of her back. When she passes, the old ones sigh. She is so like her mother.

# AND ALL THE LAND
# BETWEEN THEM

*"When she came [to him], she induced him to ask*
*her father for some property. She dismounted from*
*her donkey, and Caleb asked her,*
*'What is the matter?' She replied,*
*'Give me a present, for you have given me away as*
*Negeb-land; give me springs of water.'*
*And Caleb gave her Upper and Lower Gulloth."*
Judges 1:14-15

———————◆———————

I n the days of the conquest, after the generation of the
wandering had passed from the earth, the borders
were still being mapped, and men rushed out to van-
quish the peoples of the land. Caleb, spy, revered leader,

resolute warrior, came into the City of Arba, home to the giants of the hills. Each man there stood twice as tall as the Judeans. Each woman was broader across the hips than her Israelite sisters. The children, it has been said, were the size of grown men.

In the days of old they had been feared, but Caleb strode through the city, his sword sharpened to a murderous point. The battle was short, and Caleb victorious. He cut the giants down. The ground shook with the impact as each monstrous body fell.

When it was over, the Judeans rushed through the alleyways and courtyards, taking the houses as their own. Caleb surveyed all he had wrought and was pleased. He claimed the largest compound for himself, installed his wife and concubines, his many fine sons, and one beloved daughter, whom he had named Achsah after the gentle chimes of the bracelets that circled women's ankles. She was as beautiful as the almond trees, as graceful as the gazelles who bound through the length of the wadis. Her laugh rang like bells in a doorway as the breeze moves them. Her hair flowed like water over wet rocks.

After the City of Arba fell to him, and the last survivors of the giants had been driven from the city, Caleb called the Judean elders to dine with him in his new home. They came from north and south, east and west, to witness their people's latest victory. When they arrived, Caleb opened the gates and his arms to them.

"Welcome to the new home of Judah," he said, his voice resounding off the distant hills. Then, proud homeowner, he showed them the great extent of his domain. He took them into the houses, whose ceilings seemed to recede above their heads as if to the height of the sky. He displayed the grain silos, which were so wide a man could not see around them to the other side. Finally, he led them up to the highest roof in all of the City of Arba, swept his arm in an arc that took in all the countryside. Green fields of grain stretched out in every direction.

"All this and more is ours, my brothers," he said, and he was content. His family prospered. His wives still gave him pleasure. His sons had grown to be fierce warriors. His daughter's wisdom was revered throughout the land. He had lived a long life, had battled on behalf of God and his tribe, and now, in the fullness of his years, he could enjoy the fruits of his labor. Everywhere his eye fell gave proof to his great achievements. Every inch, every acre, every bubbling stream and well that watered the great expanse of farmland belonged to him.

He looked to the north, where his sheep and goats fed off the scrub that lined the sides of the pebbled mountain. He looked to the south, where the grass grew green and thick. Two blue veins bowed and circled the land. The water there glinted in the sun's reflection.

Just as Caleb was basking in the delight of his great accomplishment, he caught sight of something between where he stood and the verdant fields below. Distance made it look small. To Caleb's eyes it appeared as a modest square of limestone chiseled by a human hand. It was the only thing not made by God within the span of his vision.

"What is that?" he asked.

"It is Debir, my Lord," said one of Caleb's advisors. "A Canaanite city."

That evening, as the elders of Judah gathered with him to feast, Caleb sat, surrounded by family and clan, distracted and deep in thought. His mind was clouded. His sleep, he knew, would be disturbed until everything in the landscape belonged to him. Debir would have to be subdued. But Caleb had grown weary of battle. He had done his duty. It was his time to rest. Someone else would have to go take the town.

While the men around him ate, drank, and rejoiced, Caleb surveyed the room, his eyes alighting on his kinsmen from far and near. He saw how sturdy the young men had grown, how capable and enthusiastic.

Caleb's brow cleared. He ate and drank. His laugh joined again with the other sounds of merriment. He had found a solution.

At the end of the meal, when the men had filled their bellies with meat and wine, Caleb rose. He called his daughter to come stand next to him and addressed his guests.

"Brothers, cousins, kinsmen," he said. "We have all seen how God has given this land into our hands. We have gone from victory to victory. But right here, in the midst of our joy, lies proof that the work is not yet complete. Today, we saw that our dominion does not extend even as far as our eyes can see."

Achsah, called away from the women, stood beside him. Silently, she wondered why her father required her presence by his side. What had talk of war and conquest to do with her?

"I propose, therefore, a contest. Whichever man among those gathered can defeat Debir will have my daughter, Achsah, as his wife."

A cheer went up among the men. As is well known throughout the land, Judeans liked nothing better than a challenge that pitted one man against another. More than that, each man imagined himself sitting by Caleb's right hand, his treasured son-in-law. The elders called their families around them. Sons huddled tight around their fathers. Whispers filled the firelit air as champions were chosen. Arguments flared between brothers anxious to claim the glory of the challenge and were quickly quenched. Only Achsah, the object of the men's desire, did not exult.

Her eyes went black. Her voice came low and hard.

"Did you not think to consult me before making such a rash promise?" she said out of the side of her mouth. "Because of your vow, I will be tethered to one of these men, no matter if he be wise or foolish, good or mean-spirited. Do you account me so little that it doesn't matter what manner of man my husband will be?"

All around them young men argued as they jockeyed for favor with their elders. No one paid mind to the impassioned debate that raged between Caleb and his daughter.

"Daughter, be still," he said. "I have given my oath. It cannot be rescinded. Besides, the men in this room are the best among us. You should be grateful. I am guaranteeing you a hero for a husband."

Caleb felt wounded. He had thought his idea perfect—his daughter would be married to a great warrior among the people, and Debir would be his. He had already begun to imagine tearing down its buildings, stone by stone, until it was just another pile of rock on the hillside. Then, nothing would impede his view of the vast property he owned. In just a few words, his daughter had ruined his great moment.

"Will his heroism keep me warm at night?" Achsah demanded. "Will it fill my plate? Will it keep his eyes from wandering to every passing bosom or backside that comes into view?"

Caleb didn't have time to answer, for at that moment,

the first aspirant to Achsah's hand stepped forward. He was a mountain of a man who stood a head taller than anyone else and twice as wide. The giants' quarters they now occupied seemed built to hold him while the rest of them scuttled around his knees.

"See," said Caleb to Achsah, as if nature itself had just offered proof that he was right. "This is the finest specimen of a man."

"I have seen him among the others," Achsah said. "He wrestles them to the ground, then sits on their chests until the breath is almost out of them. He laughs the whole time, while under him men squirm. His bulk is all that recommends him. There was not enough matter left over in his making to fill his brain."

But Caleb exulted. Surely this colossus of a man would bring back news of Debir's defeat.

He was destined to be disappointed. Early the next morning, the man led a small group out of the City of Arba in the direction of Debir. Everyone, from Caleb to the smallest child, waited expectantly for this first challenger's successful return.

That night, the few who remained alive of the band that had left in such high spirits hobbled back into the city, their shoulders bowed in defeat. Even the champion, who had appeared so massive just one day earlier, looked shrunken and small. Debir remained untaken. The people of the City of Arba groaned. Only

Achsah was pleased. She sighed in relief at what her life could have been had this first contender succeeded.

That night, the next challenger presented himself. His nose and chin were like spear heads, thin triangles that ended in needled points. He wore a sly look on his face and watched the world as if with a sidelong glance.

Once again, Caleb turned to his daughter. "This one will surely have more success than the last. Where brute strength failed, his cunning will prevail."

"And if it does," Achsah replied, "I will live as a cunning man's wife, never sure if his next cruel trick will be played on me."

Achsah was spared that fate. The next morning, all the assembled of Judah gathered again to see this second group set off. When evening came, no one returned at all. Debir still lay untouched in the distance.

Finally, a third man stepped forward. He looked neither strong nor crafty. No muscles popped off his arms to indicate great strength. No sword hung at his side to show that he was already skilled in battle. There was nothing, in fact, that distinguished him at all other than a quiet assurance that spoke of self-regard, but not necessarily achievement.

"Is this what it has come to?" Achsah asked her father. "This man does not look like he could defeat a house cat, much less an entire city."

Even Caleb, who had brought this multitude of

kinsmen into his town, didn't remember this young man. "State your name," he said.

"Othniel son of Kenaz," the young man replied.

"And you think you can be successful where the others have failed?"

"I do."

Achsah listened carefully. She had watched the other two aspirants with growing unease. Trapped by her father's promise, she had feared that they were the best she could expect of a man. Beside her, Caleb also paid close attention, because he was growing tired of waiting for victory.

"Why is that?" Caleb asked.

"Because I have studied the others' mistakes, and I will not repeat them."

"Very well, Othniel son of Kenaz, I wish you better luck than those who came before you."

Unlike the others, Othniel didn't wait until morning. Without delay, he called his men to him and set off, cloaked in the night's deep shadows.

Achsah took notice. "Perhaps he has learned from the errors of those who went before him," she said to her father as the men slipped out of the City of Arba in the direction of Debir. Achsah felt a small hope stir in her that this man would be wiser than the rest.

"I fear you are wrong," Caleb said, with a sad shake of his head. "I have gone to war in this land many times.

God cannot make the sun stand still for us if it does not shine at all."

The night passed sleepless for those in the City of Arba. The sun rose, and still Othniel did not return. The hours passed. The sun made its passage through the sky, and fell toward the west, and still he did not return.

It was only as the last rays of the day clung to the mountains that Othniel and his men came back.

"Debir is yours," he said to Caleb. "We have taken it from the Canaanites."

———◆———

There was jubilation in the City of Arba that night and into the next morning. Caleb led his people, singing and dancing, through valleys and over hills to see Debir's desolation firsthand. As they left, Achsah climbed to the top of the highest building, where her father had stood only days before. She watched the column of men, women, and children pass through the southern gate. When they had gone, and all she heard was the echo of their song, she looked to the east and the west, the north and the south. She knew this would never be her home again.

When Caleb returned, he fulfilled his promise. Achsah and Othniel were married that night. By noon the next day, all the Judeans who had come to behold

Caleb's great fortune left the City of Arba to return to their strongholds and homes.

Achsah and Othniel were the last to go. After the excitement and commotion of the past days, the City of Arba felt bereft of life. Caleb led his daughter as far as the city wall, and then helped her mount her donkey.

Looking down at him, she said, "I hope you know what you were doing. It's only my life that will prove you right or wrong."

The newlyweds had not gone a mile when Achsah asked, "Debir was the bride price you paid for me, but what of my dowry? What, other than the clothes I wear and the ass on which I ride, has my father sent us away with?"

Othniel stopped his donkey. "Dowry?" he said. "I never thought to ask."

Achsah sat stupefied, her mouth open in disbelief. This was the man who used intelligence to defeat Debir, but he did not think to negotiate with his bride's father before he took her as his wife. "Have you never been witness to a marriage before?" she said, incredulous.

"My father always handled that kind of thing," Othniel said.

I've ended up with a dolt after all, Achsah thought. "If you weren't ready to be a man," she said, "you shouldn't have volunteered to take down an entire town."

Achsah pulled hard at the reins and turned her

donkey around. She set it back on the road to the City of Arba. "Come on."

"Where are you going?" Othniel asked.

"To get what's mine," she said.

No one was more surprised than Caleb to see the newlywed couple return so soon. "What is the matter?" he said as his daughter slipped off her donkey to confront him.

"All this is yours," she said, lifting her arm and circling it above her head, as if to take in the entire land of Judah. "You have everything you sought, yet you could not spare a single acre for me."

Both Caleb and Othniel stood silenced in the face of Achsah's vehemence.

"You are the clever one," she said to her father. "You get others to do your bidding and pay nothing in exchange. Am I like a field in the desert, worth so little that you will trade me away for nothing?

"I sat by as you bartered me away for the sake of your own holdings. I paid the debt held by your promise." She sneered. "And all I got in exchange is a hero. You have done me a great wrong. Now make it right."

"What would you have of me?" Caleb asked, because he realized that in his happiness, he may have neglected to do his duty.

Achsah looked through the gates. The great expanse of rich land spread before her. She pointed. "Give me the two springs that flow beneath Debir and all the land between them."

It was a lot to ask. She was demanding the richest farmland in all of Judah, but Achsah did not care. She foresaw a lifetime guiding Othniel as he took her father's place in the nation, and for that, she deserved as much as she desired.

Caleb heard the wisdom in all she said and all she did not say. He granted her request. Then, having accomplished her mission, Achsah led her husband out of the City of Arba again, south toward their new home.

# AUTHOR'S AFTERWORD

## THE BOOK OF RUTH

———◆———

This story begins in a bookstore. There, among the cramped fiction aisles of a local, independent shop where browsing is encouraged, I spied a slim volume wrapped in plastic. How unusual, I thought. Why, when we can rifle through Shakespeare, James Patterson, and everything in between, would anyone wrap a novel up so that potential buyers can't dip in and sample the wares?

I was intrigued. This book was off-limits, a mystery I felt compelled to solve. Despite the $35 price tag— who's crazy enough to pay $35 for a paperback work of fiction?—I circled back to it over and over, drawn as if against my will, and finally brought it up to the cashier.

It was the title that sold me: *Book of Ruth*. I had wanted to write about the biblical Book of Ruth for years, but something had always stopped me. I thought about an approach and rejected it, doubled back and thought some more. By then, I didn't even know where to start. Maybe, I thought, this writer had done what I had failed to do.

When I ripped off the plastic, I realized what had happened. It was not a novel, but a fine art book, slipped onto the fiction shelf because it did contain a made-up story of sorts. A now deceased artist, Robert Seydel, created the collage of words and images to pay homage to his late aunt, a woman named Ruth.

Here was a *Book of Ruth*, but it wasn't my Book of Ruth, the one tucked between the Song of Songs and Ecclesiastes in the Hebrew Bible. Seydel hadn't cracked the code of writing about the story of the Israelite Naomi and her loyal daughter-in-law Ruth.

That was all it took. No one was going to write the book I was looking for. I would have to do it myself.

———— ♦ ————

Of all the texts in the Hebrew Bible, the Book of Ruth is my favorite. Other tales are better known—the Garden of Eden, Moses splitting the Sea of Reeds (or the "Red Sea," as it is often translated), Samson and Delilah, but the story of Naomi and Ruth, who cling to one another in the face of loss and displacement, is one of the fullest pictures of human life in the entirety of the Hebrew Bible. It's also one of the only books in which women and women's concerns take center stage.

In traditional teachings of this book, the highlight of the story, and the reason it is read in synagogues on Shavuot (Feast of Weeks, or Pentacost, in English), is Ruth's declaration of faith:

> Do not urge me to leave you, to turn back and not follow you. For wherever you go, I will go; wherever you lodge, I will lodge; your people shall be my people, and your God my God. Where you die, I will die, and there I will be buried. Thus and more may the LORD do to me if anything but death parts me from you. (Ruth 1:16-17)

There is something poignant about Ruth's declaration. It has been pointed to over the centuries as an affirmation of the strength and beauty of Jewish beliefs. There's so much more to Ruth's words, though, and to the story in which they are set.

For one thing, this is the only place in the Hebrew Bible in which a woman declares her devotion to another woman. Ruth doesn't accept Judaism (really its precursor, since the story is set in the pre-Davidic, pre-national period) because she has been on a spiritual quest and found that the tenets of the Israelite faith speak most deeply to her. She speaks these words out of a sense of loyalty to her mother-in-law, and despite the fact that she isn't obligated to say them.

The story is fairly straightforward, at least at the beginning: a couple, Elimelech and Naomi, moves to Moab in the face of a famine in their native Judah. They live there long enough for both their sons to marry local women. Soon all three men die. In the wake of these tragedies, Naomi and her daughters-in-law, now all widowed, decide to head back to Naomi's hometown of Bethlehem. Along the way, Naomi, broken by sorrow, implores her daughters-in-law to leave her. "Turn back, each of you to her mother's house" (Ruth 1:8). It takes some convincing, but one of them, Orpah, agrees to go and turns back.

Here is the first remarkable thing about the Book of Ruth. Despite how she's been portrayed in the Talmud and many commentaries, Orpah is no villain. She stays with her mother-in-law, even after the deaths of her husband and father-in-law release her from any duty to the family she has married into. At first, she also refuses to abandon Naomi. Even returning to her family of origin is an act of devotion: Orpah doesn't want to go, but she obeys her mother-in-law's injunction.

The point is not that Orpah is a bad daughter. In

fact, there are no villains in the Book of Ruth. Rather, she is a character whose actions are determined by her situation and a reasonable sense of human psychology, a tendency that extends to all the major players in the Book of Ruth.

So we're not meant to castigate Orpah—although over the years, plenty of people have. The Babylonian Talmud, for example, records a debate in which two sages try to one-up each other in imaging just how sexually deviant Orpah was, which leaves little doubt about how negatively they viewed her. But Orpah, as depicted in the Bible, is not bad. She is a foil for Ruth. Her actions illustrate for us just how exceptional Ruth is when she chooses Naomi over her own parents.

In turning back for home, Orpah is given the chance at a comfortable life, a new marriage, the embrace of family and clan, all of which is encapsulated in Naomi's surprising choice of words when she exhorts her daughter-in-law to return not to her father, but to her "mother's house." Ruth, however, chooses to stay with Naomi. In doing so, she signs up for a life of destitution, living at the margins of an alien society, in a city and culture she does not know. What she signs up for is an existence completely interwoven with Naomi's fate.

To really understand the Book of Ruth, a reader has to be conversant with both social and legal precepts of pre-modern Israel. Most important is the fact that the story shows us an environment that leaves a widow (elderly or not) with no resources, and no ability to claim any.

When Naomi and Ruth return to Bethlehem, they are the poorest and most outcast in the city. Without husbands, they can make no claim to land, and without land, they cannot engage in commerce, or even grow food to eat.

This is the reality that Ruth accepts when she makes her famous declaration of faith, and it is even more noteworthy than the commentators and teachers who have put the focus squarely on Ruth's piety, would have it. Her pledge of allegiance to God is not a sign of religious awaking. It is proof of her dedication to Naomi. What matters in Ruth's speech is how bound up she is with her mother-in-law, and her intention to remain that way. Ruth's dedication isn't ultimately to God. That is part and parcel of her loyalty to another woman, come what may.

What comes is a life of scrounging desperation. Because Naomi is old and seemingly still immobilized by sorrow, Ruth heads out into the fields to pick up the dregs of the harvest, as illuminated in the biblical version of a safety net that commands the corners of a field be left to the beggars and paupers to take what they need to survive (Leviticus 19:9-10).

And so Ruth goes out every day to pick up the few

grains she can find to make sure that she and Naomi won't starve. It is in the course of this harvest that she comes to the notice of Boaz, the owner of the fields and a distant cousin to Naomi's late husband. Once he becomes aware of her existence, the story begins to move to its triumphant conclusion. Boaz and Ruth marry and have a son. The text even claims that Ruth is King David's great grandmother, although scholars agree that the coda containing that genealogy was added long after the story's original composition.

That coda may even account for the book's inclusion in the Hebrew Bible. Because David is the great hero and central nationalizing figure of the Hebrew Bible, and for whom very little genealogical information is given, any hint of his origins becomes important. Without those final few passages, the book is not an obvious fit with the rest of the Bible: God doesn't play an active role. No overt miracles occur. It's not about a hero or leader like Moses, Joseph, or Joshua. It doesn't have any lists of laws, such as the ones that take up so much space in Exodus and Leviticus.

The Book of Ruth diverges from the norm in other ways, too. For those interested in the women who populate the Bible, the pickings can be slim. The Hebrew Bible is a book primarily about wealthy and powerful men. When women appear, it is most often in service of the needs and goals of those men. They are the mothers

of men's children, and wives who can be reviled (Vashti), punished (Lot's wife), or simply set aside when it
is convenient for the male character to do so (Michel).
Women almost never drive national achievement. They
are more often than not relegated to supporting roles,
and even then they can go uncredited. There are so
many characters who pass only as so-and-so's wife or
daughter. They do not even merit names.

But the Book of Ruth is about women. Not just
women, but ordinary women. Even Esther, the heroine
of that titular book, is not ordinary. She is queen of
the Persian Empire, which is about as far from ordinary
as possible. She's also not the protagonist of the story.
The narrative hinges on her courage, but it is her uncle,
Mordechai, who drives the storyline.

This is why I love the Book of Ruth. It shines a
light on the female experience as it could have been,
and illuminates a behind-the-scenes reality that is dependent upon the laws men pass, but structured around
relationships that women establish between themselves.
These relationships often turn out to look nothing like
what readers of other parts of the Bible might expect.

Some of the more famous narratives about women
include Rachel and Leah, Hannah and Penina, Sarah
and Hagar. In each, the women are at odds with one
another—one can have children but is unloved, the
other is loved by their (shared) husband but barren.

These relationships, and the women themselves, are defined by jealousy. The details of these stories point to the position common to most women in the Bible, who are often important only by virtue of their sexual, emotional, and political relationships to men. They are judged based on how many children they will give to their husbands.

Like those other female figures, Ruth has a baby, but here the text deviates from the norm, as well. Boaz is the biological father, which, if this were like any other biblical story, would be the most important detail. And yet the women of the town shout with joy, "A son is born to Naomi!" Naomi, not Boaz. The infant becomes the living symbol of the fulfillment of the loyalty and love that Naomi and Ruth share through sorrow, hardship, joy, and, finally, fullness. What's more, the women of Bethlehem don't just rejoice at the baby's birth. They name him. Mothers often name their children in the Bible. This is the only instance in which the neighbors do. In the Book of Ruth, birth and rebirth become forces that bind generations and entire communities of women to one another.

Ruth is a rare text in the Bible. Not only does it revolve around women, it gives the women a real story arc, from loss to rebirth. That doesn't mean that it's radical. The Book of Ruth doesn't upend the expectations of the society it depicts. It doesn't strike out at the injustices that keep widows impoverished and powerless. Instead, it pulls back the curtain to show a side of life that is generally invisible to us, and gives its heroines a happy ending within the realities of their world.

———— ♦ ————

What does all of this have to do with this book of short stories?

Because we usually read the Bible in the context of the rabbinic and Christian traditions, we are accustomed to reading it from the perspective of the dominant male cultural and economic perspective. But there's a long history of writers taking inspiration from the stories in the Bible to illuminate it in new ways and from new perspectives. Long before John Milton turned the narrative of the creation and Christian fall into his sprawling epic poem, *Paradise Lost*, Jewish *midrash* and *agadah* contained stories that give flesh to what are often bare-bones biblical tales.

That tradition has continued in the centuries since, covering both the Hebrew Bible and the Christian New Testament. Novels and poems have been written from the viewpoint of Eve, Cain, Mary, and Jesus. I've given a lot of thought to all of them. This book is the result of decades of immersion in biblical stories. The product of a Jewish Day School education, I went on to write a doctoral dissertation on the way American poets have re-envisioned the biblical story of the creation and expulsion from the Garden of Eden. In the years since, I have taught the literary/historical approaches to the Hebrew Bible at different colleges and universities. I am lucky enough to have been exposed to both traditional, rabbinic interpretive methods and Western scholarship about the Bible.

When I set out to write the stories that make up this book, I imagined myself into characters and situations that are well known by dint of being in the most popular book ever published, but from an angle that, I suspect, most have never considered. To do so, I established a few ground rules for myself. The most important is that, while I allowed myself to play with details of the narratives, the endings could not change: Abel had to die, Sodom had to burn, Michel had to be taken back to David.

It's a sad fact that the Book of Ruth is unusual in the Bible for a reason I briefly mentioned above: It has a happy ending. Most biblical women—and men, for that matter—aren't as lucky as Ruth and Naomi. And while it's tempting to give the women whose stories this book tells their happily ever after, that wouldn't be true to the characters or their biblical narratives.

The other rule that guided my writing was that I couldn't, to the best of my ability, impose modern cultural expectations onto the plots or characters, even if my own position as a twenty-first-century writer inevitably influenced how I envisioned the stories. You won't see any updated stories here, in which the narratives are imported into our own contemporary environment. This book presents an imaginative engagement with the ancient world—its landscapes, relationships, and laws. The pre-modern world, biblical or otherwise, was often brutal and unfair. It followed a logic that seems foreign, even barbaric to us. There are elements of the Bible that I find personally distasteful—slavery, for example, which the Bible accepts as legitimate. As a modern person, I detest slavery in all forms, including selling young women for the sole purpose of producing children for their owners/husbands, a practice that was apparently so prevalent it is mentioned, and legislated, not once, but twice, in both Exodus and Deuteronomy. No matter my feelings, it was an element of biblical life that directly affected some women's experiences.

In writing this book, I have followed in the steps of the great midrashists and writers who preceded me. Like them, I don't mean for my small tales to supplant the Bible. History has proven (correctly, if you ask me) that the Bible retains its position in the Western imagination for good reason. I do hope to give a different perspective on narratives that may have become static in our reading of them.

Which leads me back to the Book of Ruth. You won't find a fictionalized version of Ruth and Naomi's story in this book. Because, while some might accuse a writer of arrogance if she dares to use the Bible as the source of her own creative production, I know when not to mess with perfection. And the Book of Ruth really is a perfect little gem, worthy of study and consideration, but too good for the likes of me to take on.

As for that other *Book of Ruth*, the "novel" I bought by mistake: as it turns out, I didn't spend my money unwisely. Thirty-five dollars is surely a lot of money for a mislabeled paperback, but it's not much when you consider that it got me thinking and writing, and prodded me to finally give voice to the stories I have to tell. It gave me, in the end, the pages you hold in your hands.

# ACKNOWLEDGMENTS

This book owes its existence to people and institutions that have impacted many phases of my life. My gratitude goes out first to my all my teachers, from my earliest years through college, graduate school, and beyond. They have taught me how to read carefully, delve deeply into any topic or endeavor, and have pushed me to expand my own understanding. I include among them all the biblical scholars whose work I have mined for years as a student and teacher, whether I have met them in person or not. Their scholarship and insights have affected the way I read, teach, and think about the Bible and so much more.

I'd like to thank Susan Weidman Schneider, Yona Zeldis McDonough, Naomi Danis, and everyone at *Lilith* magazine, which featured an abridged version of "Lot's Wife" in the Summer 2014 issue. Thank you to J. Ryan Stradal and *The Nervous Breakdown* for featuring an excerpt of "Drawn from the Water," and to Jim Ruland for his enthusiasm and support of my writing.

My thanks also go to the Jewish Publication Society, whose translation of the biblical texts I have used extensively over the years, and from which I have taken the passages that introduce every story. Because I was using a translation, issues of spelling inevitably come up, especially when it comes to the way Hebrew names are rendered in English. For ease of reading, I have chosen to use alternate spellings for the names of a few of the characters. Other than that, the translations that appear here are faithful to the JPS text.

I can't thank Patty O'Sullivan and Colleen Dunn Bates at Prospect Park Books enough for believing in the potential of this book and for helping me see it through to completion. They are a dream to work with, and I feel lucky to have had been able to do so.

My deepest thanks to Miriam Heller Stern and the Graduate Center for Education at the American Jewish University, where I taught Hebrew Bible for four years. My time preparing classes and engaging with my students, each of whom helped me learn more about the subject than I did before starting, was instrumental in allowing the ideas that grew into these stories to germinate and grow. It is no exaggeration to say that without the time I spent at AJU this book could not have been written.

Many individuals have helped me along the way. Although I wrote all the stories in this collection within the last year, the seed was planted many years ago in partnership with Leilani Riehle. The end product is very different than what we cooked up, but I am so grateful for the time we spent chewing over some of this material together. I'd like to thank David Hochman,

Michael Ellenberg, Esther Kustanowitz, Aimee Bender, Taffy Brodesser-Akner, Jeff Zack, and Rebecca Kobrin for their support and advice. Diana Reiss kept me moving, despite long hours in front of the computer. I thank her and so does my back. Michelle Fellner was so gracious and enthusiastic about creating the book trailer. It looks great, which is all thanks to her expertise. Thanks also to Matt Duncan for building my website. Many thanks to Rachel Levin, Maggie Flynn, Elline Lipkin, Kalee Thompson, Rob Kutner, Michael Becker, and Tal Kastner for reading early drafts of some of these stories. Michael Green not only continues to give me some of the best advice I get, but was an early advocate of this project, encouraging me to pursue it before I was even ready to do so.

This book would be nowhere without Ron Hart—incredible husband, first reader, steadfast cheerleader, lousy title generator. Thank you for hounding me until I turned one story into two, and then didn't let up until I had a manuscript in my hands.

Finally, to my daughters, Anina and Lula. I have been writing since I was a child, but it was only in becoming a mother that I found my voice as a writer. Athough I probably won't let them read it for many years, this book is for them.

# ABOUT THE AUTHOR

Michal Lemberger's nonfiction and journalism have appeared in *Slate, Salon, Tablet,* and other publications, and her poetry has been published in a number of print and online journals. A story from *After Abel* was featured in *Lilith* magazine. Lemberger holds an MA and PhD in English from UCLA and a BA in English and Religion from Barnard College. She has taught the Hbrew Bible as Literature at UCLA and the American Jewish University. She was born and raised in New York and now lives in Los Angeles with her husband and two daughters. This is her first collection of fiction.